She was conscious of the heat from his arm gently seeping into her, and as he moved closer she felt the brush of his long body next to hers.

It was a good feeling, that warmth of human contact, and it occurred to her that it had been a long time since she had known such tenderness. She had a strange yearning to lean against him, to have him hold her and comfort her.

This was Jake, a man she had known for barely two weeks, and instinct told her that she ought to be keeping him at arm's length. It was a pity her heart wasn't listening. Instead, it was beating out its own erratic rhythm, and seemed to be recklessly bent on overriding common sense.

A soft breeze stirred the air, and she looked out over the water. Moonlight glittered on its surface, beautiful in its serenity.

'Are you cold?' Jake asked, and she was suddenly reminded that they were standing out here on the dock, with her wearing little more than a cotton shift.

She shook her head. 'No, but I should go and put something on—a robe, or something.'

His mouth curved. 'You don't need to do that on my account. I'm perfectly happy for you to stay as you are... You feel very soft and cuddlesome to me, and you look like an angel—a dazzling white angel who makes the moonbeams dance on the water.'

When **Joanna Neil** discovered Mills & Boon®, her lifelong addiction to reading crystallised into an exciting new career writing Medical™ Romance. Her characters are probably the outcome of her varied lifestyle, which includes working as a clerk, typist, nurse and infant teacher. She enjoys dressmaking and cooking at her Leicestershire home. Her family includes a husband, son and daughter, an exuberant yellow Labrador and two slightly crazed cockatiels. She currently works with a team of tutors at her local education centre, to provide creative writing workshops for people interested in exploring their own writing ambitions.

Recent titles by the same author:

HAWAIIAN SUNSET, DREAM PROPOSAL
NEW SURGEON AT ASHVALE A&E
POSH DOC, SOCIETY WEDDING
HOT-SHOT DOC, CHRISTMAS BRIDE

THE SECRET DOCTOR

BY
JOANNA NEIL

First published in Great Britain 2010
Large Print edition 2011
Harlequin Mills & Boon Limited,
Eton House, 18-24 Paradise Road,
Richmond, Surrey TW9 1SR

© Joanna Neil 2010

ISBN: 978 0 263 21720 9

Harlequin Mills & Boon policy is to use papers that are
natural, renewable and recyclable products and made
from wood grown in sustainable forests. The logging and
manufacturing process conform to the legal environmental
regulations of the country of origin.

Printed and bound in Great Britain
by CPI Antony Rowe, Chippenham, Wiltshire

THE SECRET DOCTOR

CHAPTER ONE

THE house was just as Lacey remembered it. Several years had gone by since she had last set foot on the property on Florida's Lower Keys, but now, as she gazed around, overwhelming feelings of familiarity and nostalgia besieged her.

The building stood two storeys high, with decking on both levels so that people could sit outside and look out over the bay while taking in the warm subtropical air. The hurricane shutters were folded back right now, revealing an abundance of windows and glass doors that would flood the house with light.

The whole structure was long and wide, its clean lines white-painted, so that it appeared picture perfect against the vivid blue of the sky. In the distance, coconut palms dipped their branches towards the sand, swaying lightly in the faint breeze.

Tears sprang to Lacey's eyes as the memories came flooding back…those long, hot summers of her teenage years, when she would run along the beach with her sister Grace, or swim in the warm waters of the sea. They were happy memories, of a time when the two girls had idled away their vacations in natural pursuits, while their parents had relaxed in their holiday home.

'It'll be so good to see you again,' Grace had said over the phone just last week. 'I can't wait to come down and visit once you're settled in. But…' Grace paused. 'Won't this be a huge change for you? Are you quite sure you've thought it all through properly? I mean, you've lived in the UK all your life, and leaving all that behind will surely be quite a wrench? It was different for me. I had no choice but to come to the States, being married and with the children and all… I just went where Matt's job took him. I'm longing to be able to see you more often, but are you quite sure you're ready to put down roots here?'

That was something Lacey had thought about, long and hard, over these last few months. Some two years had passed since their parents had died, but finally the house in the UK had been sold, and Lacey had to come to terms with all the changes that had taken place in her world. What was she going to do with the rest of her life?

Of course, things might have been different if she hadn't split up with Nick, her long-term boy-friend. Once they had drifted apart, life had lost its rosy glow, and all she had been able to think of was being somewhere closer to Grace. *Family*, that was it, that was what mattered most of all.

She braced herself, trying to shake off those melancholy thoughts. Maybe she was simply tired after her long journey. The sun was setting now, casting a golden glow over the horizon, and she took one last look at the exterior of the house before turning the key in the lock of the front door.

She would have gone directly to the kitchen, to switch on the kettle and make herself a reviving cup of coffee, but the tranquillity of the evening was suddenly shattered by the intermittent sounds of banging, as though someone was hammering away at some solid, impenetrable object. The noise filled the air, an abominable intrusion that grated on her nerves.

She frowned. Who on earth was making that awful racket? Hadn't Rob said that her neighbour would be away for the rest of this week? Something had to be wrong. Was the place next door being burgled…ransacked?

She dropped her suitcases in the hall and went out of the house, doing her best to locate where the disturbance was coming from. They were isolated out here, some distance from any other houses, so it had to be her neighbour's place that was under threat.

The secluded nature of her surroundings made her stop and think for a moment. Ought she to take some sort of defensive weapon with her—a

broom handle, maybe, or a heavy fire extin-
guisher? But perhaps she was overreacting?

Instead, she ran her fingers over the touchpad
of the mobile phone that was clipped to her belt.
She could speed-dial for help if necessary.

In the distance, she saw what looked like a
barn, a huge building, its doors standing open,
and there was light coming from inside. She
walked towards it, taking the path that followed
the line of the dock, and all the while the banging became louder and louder.

When she reached the barn, she stopped at
the doorway. A man was in there, working,
his long body leaning over what looked like a
huge upturned boat that was in the process of
being built. The hull was made up of golden
oak-coloured planking, and the smell of new
wood filled the barn.

There was no banging now. He was running
his hand with infinite care along a seam line, as
though testing for flaws in the woodwork, and
Lacey could see that his fingers were strong,

but not weathered by manual work as she might have expected. His skin was lightly sun bronzed, and his forearms were covered with a smattering of dark hair.

He hadn't noticed that she was standing there, and for a moment Lacey watched him in fascination. He was wearing dark blue jeans that showed off the taut, muscular lines of his long legs, and above that he had on a white T-shirt. He was in his mid-thirties, she guessed, a man who obviously kept himself fit, judging from his broad shoulders and rippling biceps.

Her absorbed reverie came to a swift end as the banging started up once more, with ear-shattering intensity. He had picked up a mallet and was pounding it against the head of a metal tool, driving some kind of thick cotton padding between the planks of the boat.

She covered her ears with her hands and walked fully into the barn. 'Hello, there,' she said, striving to make herself heard above the din.

His reaction wasn't quite what she had

expected, but it was clear that she had startled him. He dropped the metal tool, which clanged as it hit the floor, but the mallet continued on its way, driving home with brute force and landing directly on his thumb.

The mallet joined its partner tool on the ground as the man gave a sharp yelp of pain. He hopped round in a circle of agony and the air was filled with an explosion of indecipherable expletives, ground out through gritted teeth.

Lacey's jaw froze in dismay. Guilt ripped through her as she watched him hold his injured hand in an effort to numb the pain with his fingers. His thumb was visibly beginning to swell, and the blood was building up underneath the nail bed, turning it to a dark shade of purple. She could only imagine the throbbing intensity of the pain.

He bent double for a moment or two, and then straightened, fixing her with a dazed stare. They stood in silence for a while, facing one another, until gradually his gaze sharpened on her.

'Who are you?' he said. 'What are you doing here?' Then he frowned. 'I had no idea anyone was within a mile of this place.'

'That's what I thought, too.' Lacey looked him over, doubt bringing a crooked line to crease her brow. 'Rob told me my neighbour would be away this week, so I came to find out what was going on. With all that noise, it sounded as though someone was wrecking the place.'

He winced, holding onto his hand as though the pain was getting to him. The colour was beginning to drain from his face. 'Yes, Rob was right. I was supposed to be attending a business meeting in Miami, but it fell through.'

'Oh, I see.' She hesitated, her gaze troubled as she took in the extent of the damage. 'I'm sorry I intruded on you and caused you to hit your hand.' If she hadn't butted in, he wouldn't have hurt himself, would he? It also occurred to her that this wasn't exactly the best way to meet her new neighbour for the very first time.

He straightened, bracing his shoulders. 'At

least you were trying to keep an eye on things. I hope you'll forgive the language.' Now that he had overcome the initial shock of injury, his voice was returning to an even keel, a deeply satisfying masculine timbre, firm and charismatic.

'Please don't worry about it,' she murmured, a wave of remorse for what she had done washing over her. For his part, he was still staring at her, his blue-grey eyes piercing in intensity, as though he was aiming to take in every detail of her slender shape.

Lacey was all too conscious of his glance roaming over her. She was wearing a cream-coloured linen skirt, cool and comfortable for the climate, teamed with a pale magenta cotton top. Both garments clung where they touched, and that made his slow, thorough scrutiny all the more uncomfortable to bear.

She shrugged back her long, honey-blonde hair and fixed him in return with an unwavering, blue-eyed stare. Her feelings of guilt were beginning to recede a little. She had been out of order, walking in on him, an innocent man on his own property, but he had been creating an almighty din and she had had just cause to investigate.

'I'm Jake Randall,' he said. 'Normally, I'd offer to shake your hand but, given the circumstances, I think I'll give it a miss this time.' His mouth made a wry, pained twist that managed to light up his features and add a roguish quality to his half-smile. He was still supporting his injured thumb with his free hand.

'Lacey Brewer,' she told him. 'I'm moving into the house along the dock.'

He nodded. 'I wasn't expecting you to arrive yet. Rob said you would be coming over some time next weekend. I think he was warning me to be on my best behaviour.'

'Oh! Was he really?' She blinked. She wasn't quite sure how she ought to respond. 'I can't imagine why he would think it necessary to do that.'

She knew, though, that Rob had reservations

about his next-door neighbour. Rob was an old friend, a reliable tenant who had been living in the house for the last couple of years while she decided what to do with the property. He had her best interests at heart, and she was well aware that he had his doubts about Jake Randall. Last time she had spoken to Rob, though, he had come to the conclusion that her neighbour was, at best, slightly eccentric.

'He left for the Everglades a couple of days ago,' Jake said, 'off on another of his filming expeditions. Or, at least, he was heading out there after a detour to visit his family. He made it clear to me that if I saw you around the place you had a right to be there and I should give you some space.' He gave her a thoughtful look. 'He seems to be very protective of you.'

She smiled, pleased to know that Rob was looking out for her. 'We've known each other a long time. He was right, though, I wasn't sup-posed to be here until next weekend, but I had a change of plans. My boss discovered I had some days owing to me so I finished my contract at the hospital where I was working earlier than expected and caught a different flight. It will give me a chance to settle in and take some time off before I have to start work again.'

'Hmm… Rob told me that you're a doctor…is that right?' His dark brows lifted in a querying fashion, and she noted that they were the exact colour of his hair, raven black, lending him a devilish look that was emphasised by the strongly sculpted lines of his face…a face that was taut at the moment with the effort of containing his pain. 'Emergency medicine, he said.'

She nodded, and then glanced briefly at his hand. 'That's right. You know, I think perhaps you ought to have that thumb treated. You're growing paler by the minute, and I can see that it's troubling you a lot. It happens when the blood keeps pumping beneath the nail, building up pressure because it has nowhere else to go.' She tried to gauge his reaction, just as she would have done if he were a patient back in the UK, and his wince told her everything she needed to know. 'I have a medical bag back at the house,' she told him. 'I could treat your injury for you and do something to relieve the pain, if you like.'

He thought about it for a moment, as though trying to weigh up his options. 'Okay. Thanks. I guess that would be as good a way as any to get to know my new neighbour.'

He stowed his tools away in a box and then secured the door of the barn, before setting off with her along the dock. A couple of boats were moored there, a yacht and a schooner, and further along the wharf there was a collection of lobster pots.

The fresh smell of the sea wafted on the warm breeze, filling Lacey's senses, and planting a seed of hope for the future. She had come away from all that she had ever known to start afresh and what better place could she hope to do that than here?

Back at the house, she showed him into her

kitchen. 'You should sit down,' she said. 'You look as though you're about to pass out.' Faint beads of perspiration were starting to form on his forehead. She glanced surreptitiously at his wounded thumb. He ought to have an X-ray, in case anything was broken, but her immediate priority was to lessen his pain. 'Just give me a minute,' she said. 'I'll go and get my medical bag.'

'Thanks.' He took a seat by the glass-topped table in the breakfast area.

When she came back into the room a moment later, she set to work straight away, laying out her swabs and dressings on a clean plastic surface and pulling on a pair of surgical gloves.

'First of all, I'm going to paint the nail with povidone iodine solution to make sure that any bacteria that might be present are killed. Then I'm going to heat up a metal paper clip over the gas hob to sterilise it. I'll put the tip of the paper clip into the base of your nail and the heated metal will burn a hole through the nail and allow the blood to escape.' She looked at him. 'Are you going to be okay with that?'

'If you told me you were going to hack off my thumb with a machete, I'd probably be okay with it right now,' he said, his square jaw clamping. 'Just do what you have to do.'

She smiled softly at his terse response, and proceeded with the operation. 'This shouldn't hurt,' she said. 'You should feel instant relief when the hole is opened up.' She removed the paper clip as soon as the blood began to spurt, and he took over from her then, mopping up with the swabs as the wound oozed.

'Phew,' he managed after a while. 'That is so much better. Thank you. I owe you.'

'You're welcome.' She bundled the paper clip and used swabs into a plastic bag and threw them into the nearby bin. 'As soon as the bleeding stops, I'll apply an antibiotic ointment and cover it with a dressing strip. Keep it dry for a couple of days...and you ought to go and get an X-ray, just in case anything is broken.'

'I doubt that will be necessary,' he said. 'All they'll do is give me a finger splint to make it more comfortable and charge my insurance company for the privilege.'

She acknowledged that with a nod. Things were different over here in the States. Medical services had to be paid for on the spot. It was a very different system from the one in the UK.

'You'll probably lose your fingernail,' she warned him, 'but it will grow back in about six months.'

He gave a soft laugh. 'I don't mind losing such a tiny part of me,' he said. 'Here, let me help tidy up.' He took over from her, and she went over to the sink to wash her hands.

'Rob said he had stocked up on provisions for me before he left,' she said, going over to the fridge and peering inside. 'I can offer you orange juice, or coffee, if you prefer?'

'Coffee sounds great.' He looked around the kitchen while she added coffee grounds to the percolator. 'This all looks new,' he said in an appreciative tone, his glance taking in the pale wood of the units and the decorative glass panelling of the wall cupboards. 'I don't recall any of this. Last time I was here, there was an old kitchen range and oak units.'

'Really?' That must have been some time ago, before her parents had bought the place, Lacey guessed. Perhaps he'd dropped by every now and again to visit whoever had owned the house back then. Clearly, Rob hadn't invited him in but, then, Rob tended to be a very private person.

He nodded and continued to gaze around the room. It was a spacious kitchen, well set out in a U-shaped formation, with a breakfast area at one end by the French doors. Beyond those was decking that looked out over the orange grove and distant mangroves. 'I suppose you must have had it remodelled. This house is quite a few years old, isn't? Though you wouldn't know it to look at it.'

'Yes, it is. My parents bought it about twelve

years ago, but I believe it was built long before that. Around fifty years or more, I should imagine.' She smiled briefly. 'It has certainly stood the test of time. As to the kitchen, I remember the old one but my mother had it modernised some three years ago, along with the rest of the house. My parents used to come here whenever they could. My father worked for a shipping company, and his job took him all over the world, but my parents always tried to make it back here for the holidays—they would stay here for several weeks during the summer months.'

His gaze was pensive. 'I was probably in Miami during those years. My parents moved next door when I was away at university, and I only came back here to stay some eighteen months ago. They passed on some time ago and my brother kept an eye on the place until he had to go to work in Jacksonville.'

'I'm sorry—about your parents, I mean. I know what it's like to lose family.' She was quiet for a moment or two, her thoughts dwelling on the events of the past.

Then she dragged her mind back to the present. Jake's absence in Miami would most likely explain why they had never met.

She poured the coffee and then pushed the mug towards him. 'Help yourself to cream and sugar.' She frowned as she checked the contents of the fridge and freezer. 'I'm starving. All I've had to eat today is the meal on the plane, but it looks as though Rob has left me a choice of quick snacks. I could rustle up some empanadas if you're interested?' Getting to know the new neighbour worked both ways, and this seemed like an opportunity not to be wasted.

'Wow. The girl next door is turning out to be full of incredible talents…emergency medicine, culinary arts…' His blue-grey eyes took on a gleam of mischief. 'And she looks good, too. Seems to me things are definitely looking up.'

'I wouldn't get too far ahead of yourself, if I were you,' she retorted in a dry tone, switching on the oven and reaching into the freezer for a stack of pastry shells. 'You haven't tasted my cooking yet. Anyway, the pastry's the supermarket frozen variety.' She separated the pastry discs onto a piece of parchment paper. 'Besides, considering that I was on my way over to your place to investigate the disturbance, we may still end up having our disagreements. I can't say I'm a fan of late-night noise.'

His mouth made a crooked shape. 'I'm sorry about that. I wanted to work on the boat, and I felt pretty secure in thinking that I wouldn't be disturbing anyone, with Rob away from home. Wrongly, as it turns out.'

'It looks like a big project. Have you done it all yourself?' Lacey started to prepare the fillings for the empanadas, layering strips of chicken, bacon and cheese on top of the pastry.

'Yes, all of it. It's just a hobby. There's something incredibly satisfying about working with wood…the smell, the feel of it, the finished product.'

'What wood are you using? Oak's a good hardwood, isn't it?'

He nodded. 'It is. Actually, I've been using a variety of wood-oak for the timbers and floors, cedar for the planks. The inwales, thwart risers and sheer strakes are larch.'

She had been folding the pastry into little dough packets, crimping the edges, but now she paused, giving him a long look from under golden lashes. 'I beg your pardon?'

'Sorry.' He grinned. 'It all gets a bit technical and I get carried away sometimes. Boat building tends to bring out the fanatic in me.'

Her mouth made a faint upward curve. 'So I see.' She placed a baking tray, loaded with empanadas, into the hot oven. 'I'm not sure I understood quite what you were doing back there, hammering thick cotton wadding between the planks.' She rubbed her hands on a clean towel and lifted the mug of coffee to her lips, taking a satisfying swallow. Then she arched her spine and rubbed at a knot of tension in the small of her back. It had been a long day.

He watched her, his gaze moving languorously over her, stroking her feminine curves, a flicker of interest darting in the blue depths of his eyes.

Lacey straightened. She knew that entirely male look, and she was suddenly all too conscious of her actions. The last thing she needed was to have him pay her that much attention. She was through with men, at least relationship-wise. They complicated things, promised the earth and a lifetime of love and then let you down when things didn't go their way.

Jake smiled. 'They call it caulking.'

She frowned. 'Caulking?' For a second or two, she had completely lost the drift of their conversation. The plain truth was the male of the species was a liability. You never knew where you were with them. And this man was probably no exception. He was only here in her kitchen because he had set her on a path of investigation.

'Think of it as padding,' he said helpfully, and she struggled to bring her thoughts under control once more. 'The material fills in the wedge between the planks and makes sure that they don't move…they swell, of course, or shrink, depending on different levels of moisture. You need a boat to be watertight as well as mechanically sound, so I'll apply a coat of epoxy resin, and then I'll paint it.'

'Oh, I see.' At least, she thought she did. Whatever procedures he was following, he was building a good-looking boat back there in his barn. 'You already have a couple of boats moored alongside the dock, as far as I could see. Do you collect them? What's this one for?'

'Lobster fishing. As to the others, they were inherited from my father and my grandfather. I guess you could say that boats and the sea are part of my heritage.' He gave her a crooked smile, and for some reason she had the idea that it was an ironic kind of smile, as though he was holding something back. Perhaps Rob had been right when he'd said that Jake was not quite like other men. There was a hidden side to him, Rob had said, a part of him that you couldn't quite fathom.

The scent of hot cheese and bacon filled the kitchen, and she pulled herself together and went to check the oven.

'These are done,' she said. 'You'll have to mind that you don't burn your tongue. We don't want you being injured for a second time today, do we?'

'Oh, I don't know about that…you make a very lovely medic.' He gave her a wickedly sexy glance that immediately set her temperature rising. 'You can tend to my injuries any day.'

'I wouldn't count on that, if I were you,' she said dryly, 'or on anything else, for that matter. I can see when I'm being strung a line.' She figured it was better to cut him down at the first pass, rather than leave things to roll on and get out of hand. She slid golden pasties onto a plate and passed them to him.

'That's a great shame,' he said, affecting to appear dismayed but finding it difficult to prevent a grin from breaking out. He gave a false sigh. 'I dare say I'll have to console myself with the empanadas instead.'

CHAPTER TWO

LACEY picked her way carefully along the rocky shoreline, deep in thought, her gaze sweeping along the line of coral reef islands that made up the Keys. They made a glorious picture, strung out like a jewelled, emerald bracelet across the Florida Straits. To the west the sun-dappled waters of the Gulf of Mexico gave off a blue haze as the heat of the day began to rise.

She was content for the first time in a long while, and perhaps now she would find the wherewithal to cope with whatever lay before her. A couple of weeks had passed since that evening when she had first arrived here and met up with her new neighbour, but she still wasn't quite sure what to make of him. An hour or so in Jake's company had been enough to make her realise that he was a definite threat to her peace of mind. And peace was what she wanted right now, above all.

There hadn't been any contact between them since that first day, probably because she had been out and about, exploring the island and making the most of her newfound liberty. She was still licking her wounds after the disaster of her relationship with Nick. On top of that she'd had to cope with the upheaval of selling her parents' house before the move out here. What she needed now was space, a chance to sort out her troubled thoughts. Jake was a distraction she could do without.

'Hello, there… Lacey…wait up…'

She half turned. It was almost as though thinking about Jake had conjured him up. He was heading towards her, emerging from the woods that covered the land behind both houses.

She slowed down and he came alongside her. 'So, I've found you at last,' he said, his deep voice vibrant, echoing his energetic presence. 'I've been looking for you these last few days.

Then, just now, as I was on my way to the boat-house I spotted you down here.' He fell into step beside her, sending her an oblique glance that took in her loose cotton top and the white shorts that showed off a golden expanse of long, shapely legs. 'You're looking good…' he murmured. 'All sun kissed and glowing with health. This part of the world must agree with you.'

'The climate's certainly better than it is back home,' she agreed. 'It's tempted me to get out and about while I have the chance.'

'Hmm.' His eyes took on a faint gleam. 'So much so that you're hardly ever at home. I was beginning to get the idea that you might be trying to avoid me.'

Her mouth made a wry shape. He really wasn't far wrong in thinking that way. 'As I said, I've been spending time getting to know the place all over again. It's all so different out here. I feel as though I'm being given a glimpse of paradise.'

As she spoke, a black cormorant, standing some three feet high, paused by the water's edge, where it had been searching for food, and spread its wings to dry. He lifted his orange-tinted throat towards the sun, as though he was stretching and taking joy in the day.

Jake followed her glance. 'You see a lot of them around the coastal area. You'll often catch sight of white heron, too, wading in the shallows, but they're shy and will fly off if you disturb them.'

'I know. I'll take good care not to do that,' she murmured. 'Herons are such graceful, beautiful birds, aren't they?' She glanced at him. He was casually dressed, in cargo pants and a navy T-shirt, and looked completely at ease with life in general.

He inclined his head, tilting it a little so that he could study her. 'You seem to be very interested in all that the Keys have to offer, especially the natural environment… but there are other ways to enjoy life around here, you know?' His voice softened. 'In fact, I'm going to be hosting a get-together at my place tomorrow evening. It'd be great if you could come along. Any time from seven-thirty onwards.'

Her gaze met with his. She wasn't at all sure that it would be a good idea to spend her leisure time with him. He started all kinds of warning bells ringing just by being close at hand. Even now, she could feel the warmth emanating from his long, lithe body as he moved along-side her, and her pulse had notched up a beat. She felt as though she ought to take a step away from him in a kind of desperate attempt at self-preservation.

'Thanks for the invitation,' she murmured, 'only I'm afraid I'll have to turn you down. I start my new job tomorrow, and I'll be working the late shift…for the whole of the week, as it happens. I doubt I'll be home until an hour or so before midnight.'

'You could still come along.' His voice took on a husky, coaxing note. 'The night is still young at that time on the Keys.'

'Perhaps it is for some.' She smiled. 'You get full marks for trying, anyway.'

'Hmm…' His gaze was quizzical. 'You can't blame a man for doing his best, but if it's a competition we're in, you have the highest score for caginess.'

He frowned, looking around briefly, and Lacey wondered if he was finding it a new experience, being thwarted this way. She doubted women often turned him down. He had a compelling, persuasive manner about him, and as for looks, he definitely had the wow factor. It was a pity she was immune…or should that be allergic? She had given everything to her relationship with Nick and it had turned sour. Why would she want to risk putting herself in the danger zone all over again?

She stopped walking. They had reached a clump of mangrove trees, jostling for room at the water's edge. Their gnarled, tangled roots were a reddish colour, partly submerged in the salt water so that it seemed as though the trees were walking on its surface. Small birds hovered at the water's edge, searching for morsels of food among the crustaceans. Looking up, Lacey caught a glimpse of brown pelicans nesting in the branches. As she watched, one of them flew down, splashed into the water and emerged a moment later, soaring upwards, triumphant, with a fish in its beak.

'I think we must have come as far as we can along this path,' she said, giving her attention back to Jake. 'It's time I started for home, anyway. I have to go into town for some provisions or I shall be living on stale bread and water for the rest of the week.'

He nodded, turning with her, and together they retraced their steps. 'I expect the supplies Rob left you must be running low by now.' He sent her a thoughtful glance, and then said, 'He's been away for some time, hasn't he? Are you expecting him back any day soon?'

She shook her head, frowning a little. 'I'm not sure. Actually, I'm a bit concerned about him. He went off to film a documentary for a local TV company, but when he finished there he was going to drop by my place and pick up some belongings before visiting his family. He should have been back a few days ago.'

'So you think something might have happened to him?'

'I really don't know what to think. I know he hasn't been too well of late—nothing serious, he said, but I know he's been seeing a doctor regularly over these past few months.' She frowned. 'Even so, it isn't like him not to get in touch.' She made an awkward shrug of her shoulders. 'I'm probably worrying unnecessarily. He knows how to look after himself but, there again, the Everglades can be tricky if things go wrong.'

'It could be that he had a change of plan and went straight on to his family.'

'Yes, that's most likely the answer...but I still think he would have given me a call to let me know. I haven't been able to contact him.' Perhaps she was distracted by thoughts of Rob and wasn't paying attention to where she was going, because she missed her footing just then, and stumbled over a patch of rough ground. Instantly, Jake's hand shot out, grasping her arm in a light, but firm, grip.

'Are you okay?'

She nodded. 'I'm fine, thanks.' She wished her voice sounded more certain, but quite unexpectedly his touch was beginning to play havoc with her defences. The warmth of his fingers seared her tender skin, and her whole body flamed in reaction to his nearness as he drew her close to steady her. Her mouth was suddenly dry, her heart hammering against her rib cage as his thigh brushed hers and her nervous system went into meltdown. She couldn't think straight with him holding her that way, with the flat of his hand resting on her waist, burning through the thin cotton of her top. She struggled to compose herself. 'I'll be all right now… Thanks,' she mumbled. 'I can manage.'

'Are you sure? The ground is difficult underfoot here where the coral has been left exposed by the sea.'

'I'm sure.' She straightened, as though to emphasise the point, and he released her readily enough, so that at last her head began to clear.

'You said Rob was supposed to pick up some belongings—does that mean he was going to move on from your place?'

She nodded. 'Yes, although I dare say he will come back to the Keys from time to time because he still has contacts here. He found himself an apartment in Miami, close to where the film company is based and within a short distance of his parents' and his brothers' homes, so, all in all, I imagine things have turned out quite well for him.'

'I expect so.' He was thoughtful for a moment or two. 'You told me that you'd been friends for some time… How did you two meet?'

'We met when I was doing my medical training. He was doing a completely different course—media studies—but we had both joined the camera club on campus, and we became friends. I think he decided to come back to the States because there were good opportunities here for him in the television and film industry…and of course his family were here. He was homesick, I suppose, and having spent holidays here in Florida I could talk to him about familiar places, so that's probably what drew us together in the first place.'

By now they had reached Lacey's house, and after a few more minutes of chat they parted company, with Jake heading off once more for the boathouse. 'Going by boat is the best way to explore the Keys,' he told her. 'You should let me take you out on the water some day. It'll open up a new world for you.' His look was mischievous, inviting her to take him up on the offer there and then.

'Maybe some other time. I'll think about it,' she said, taking the easy way out.

He threw her a wry smile, and she guessed he was well aware that she was prevaricating once more.

Lacey wasn't at all concerned about what he might be thinking. He would most likely forget about the offer, or at the very least he would give up trying when faced with constant rejection. That suited her fine. Jake was a complication she could do without.

Next day, she decided to eat her breakfast out on the deck. There was something utterly relaxing about sitting here first thing in the morning, she reflected, sipping freshly squeezed orange juice as she gazed out over the straits. Behind her, the glass doors to the dining room were opened wide to let the fresh, warm air sweep through the house, but here on the deck she had laid a table with a rack of toast, butter and apricot preserve. It was a perfect way to start the day.

In the far distance, boats dipped on the blue sea, moving gently with the rise and fall of the waves. Closer to home, if she looked carefully, she could make out the sand and sea grass through the clear water.

It was a view she would always delight in.

In fact, with every day that passed she found something new to persuade her that this was where she belonged. She was growing used to the leisurely pace of life out here. It suited her frame of mind and in time might help to restore order out of the confusion that had preoccupied her of late. Of course, going out to work would dampen some of that holiday feeling and leave her little time to meditate, but it was probably for the best. She needed to keep busy.

She spread a generous helping of preserve onto a slice of buttered toast and then bit into it, savouring the taste. It was strange that Jake didn't appear to have to go out to work. He'd mentioned business meetings, but what kind of business was it where he never went to the office?

She knew he was home based, because from time to time she would hear banging coming from the barn, muffled nowadays because he invariably kept the door shut. How did he stand the tropical heat? It must be like an oven in there, unless he was using a portable air-conditioner.

On other days she would see him setting out in one of the boats, heading across the bay towards the ocean. That was the life, wasn't it? Laid-back, lazy days, following whatever whim caught his fancy.

Straightening up, she sighed and quickly brushed crumbs from her fingers. Enough of thinking about her intriguing neighbour...she didn't have time to sit around here any longer dwelling on what he might or might not be up to. Her shift was due to start at the Bay View Hospital very shortly, and if she was to make a good impression on her first day, she had better look lively and get herself into gear.

An hour later she was driving along the main highway that linked the islands to one another and continued on in a long ribbon towards mainland Florida. The hospital was just a twenty-minute drive away from where she lived, and travelling there was a refreshingly smooth experience after the congested roads she was used to back in the UK.

'We're really glad to have you on board, Lacey,' Mike, the attending physician, greeted her as she walked through the doors of the emergency room. He ran a hand through his thick, dark hair and from the knot in his brow and by his general demeanour Lacey could see that he was harassed. 'We're rushed off our feet right now,' he explained, 'so after you've taken a few minutes to acclimatise yourself, we'd appreciate your help dealing with the walking wounded. Then later on in the day when Dr Mayfield, the intern, goes off duty, perhaps you could take over from him and look at the patients who've already been admitted for observation. I'll show you around properly when the pace settles down a bit.'

She smiled at his harried welcome. Not much difference there, then. It was much the same story back in London.

'Just point me in the direction of the locker

room and I'll grab a lab coat,' she told him. 'I'm sure I'll find my way around. If not, I'll ask.'

'That's great,' he said, a look of relief crossing his face. 'Welcome to Bay View. You'll find we're a friendly bunch here, and we all support one another come what may. Rick Mayfield's a good young doctor… I'm sure you'll find he'll be a great help to you. Anyway, if you have any problems at all, just shout.'

'I'll do that.' She went to the locker room to stow away her bag and jacket, and within minutes she was back on the main floor of the emergency room, checking through the list of patients waiting to be seen.

'There's a wrist fracture in treatment room one,' the assisting nurse said, 'and a shoulder dislocation in room two. You might find it easier to deal with the wrist first, while I find someone to help you with the shoulder.'

'Thanks, Emma.' The nurse was a pretty girl, with clear hazel eyes and long, chestnut-coloured hair tied back in a ponytail. She was good at her job, confident, and a fountain of knowledge about the set up in the busy emergency room. Lacey worked with her throughout what was left of the morning, and on into the afternoon.

Around teatime, when Dr Mayfield was preparing to go off duty, he came to find Lacey. He was a young man, fair haired, and, from what she had gathered, conscientious in the way he did his job.

He studied her, a wave of fair hair falling across his brow. 'How's it going today? Have you managed to find your way around our system?'

'More or less.' She smiled. 'Everyone's been great, pointing me in the right direction when I was lost, or, best of all, showing me where you stash the pasties and cakes.'

'Well, we have to get our priorities right, don't we?' He chuckled and then turned his attention to business, outlining the details of patients he had admitted for observation that day. He handed over the files. 'Anyway, best of luck with these,' he told her. 'They're mostly respiratory problems or cardiac queries.'

He made brief comments as she checked each patient's file, but Lacey hesitated at one in particular. The name and profile of the patient jumped out at her and alarm bells started to ring inside her head.

'This man—Mr Callaghan,' she murmured, scanning the text. 'It says here that he was brought in suffering from dehydration and that he appeared to be in a confused state.' She looked at the intern. 'What happened to him?'

'Apparently he was filming some alligators in the marshes and came unstuck. From what I can piece together, one of the alligators started to head towards him and he retreated, but twisted his ankle and then went off in the wrong direction instead of returning to his base. His ankle's fine, just sprained, so I've applied a compress and put on a support bandage.'

Rick ran his gaze fleetingly over the file. 'It's his general condition that's giving us cause for concern. He passed out a couple of times, and he's suffering from palpitations. According to his notes, he's been receiving treatment for cardiac arrhythmia over the past year, so that probably needs more investigation. Anyway, he has been given fluids, and he's had a bath and generally been made to feel more comfortable, but his vital signs are not too good at the moment.'

'I'll go and take a look at him straight away,' Lacey said. 'I'm sure I know him—he's a friend. He went out to the Everglades recently and didn't return.'

'Sounds as though he's had a lucky escape, then.'

She nodded, and then glanced through her list of patients once more. There was no particular urgency to any of them that she could see, so went to seek out Rob Callaghan straight away.

It was exactly as she had suspected. Rob was lying in bed, his light brown hair tousled against his pillows. He appeared to be dozing, but as she approached the bedside his eyelids flickered and he blinked, acknowledging her presence with a few mumbled words.

'Lacey,' he said in a low, cracked voice, 'it's good to see you. You're a sight for sore eyes.'

'I think I'll take that literally,' she murmured, noting the grey circles round his eyes and the general sunken appearance of his skin. 'What have you been doing to yourself?' She could see from the monitors that his blood pressure was high, and his heart rate was a lot faster than it ought to be.

'I got lost,' he said. 'There was no water, and my phone battery failed. I feel so stupid.' There was a breathless, weary quality to his voice, and she knew that she shouldn't tire him by asking too many questions.

'Well, at least you're safe now,' she murmured. 'I'm a little concerned about some of your symptoms, though. You told me some time ago that you had been having palpitations, and your ECG shows that your heart is going at full tilt right now, even after the medication Dr Mayfield gave you. I think we need to find out what's going on, so I'd like to run some tests.'

After resting in bed for the last hour or so, his symptoms should have begun to subside by now, but that clearly wasn't happening. She gave him a thoughtful, assessing glance. 'Perhaps I ought to leave you to rest. You don't look as though you're in any fit state to be talking.'

He frowned. 'Stay awhile. Do you have time to sit with me for a bit? I know you must have other patients to see.'

'Of course I can stay. There's nothing urgent to drag me away for a while.' She pulled up a chair beside his bed and placed her hand over his. 'Do your parents know that you're here? Do you want me to get in touch with anyone?'

'They're coming over. I think it took a while to contact them because they were out of town.' He studied her fleetingly. 'Florida suits you,' he said. 'I always thought you would do well out here.' He took a deep breath in order to gather strength and then added, 'How are you getting on with Jake? I'm assuming you've met?'

'Oh, yes, we've met.' Her lips made an odd shape. 'I can't quite make him out. He seems to enjoy a very relaxed way of life, and even though he talks about business meetings, I've no idea what he does for a living.'

'Nothing, right now, I guess.' Rob's mouth made a cynical line. 'He likes to party…and I mean parties… every month or so…big affairs, with his wealthy friends. He spends the rest of his time snorkelling, scubadiving, or sunbathing on board his yacht.'

Lacey's eyes widened. 'All the time?'

He nodded. 'There are maybe one or two business meetings thrown in from time to time. Perhaps he just feels he doesn't need to do any-thing more.'

Lacey shook her head. 'I imagine that could be fun for a while, but I'm not sure I could live like that all the time. My work's important to me. I'd need to do something more fulfilling with my life than sit around endlessly soaking up the sun.'

'I'm with you on that. Though, right now, lazing around sounds like the ideal occupation for me.' He made an attempt to smile, and she knew he was battling extreme fatigue.

She looked at him with concern. 'I've tired you out… I knew I shouldn't have sat down here and let you talk.'

'No.' Rob's breathing was ragged. 'I'm glad you agreed to stay. I'm only telling you these things because I know he'll make a play for you—it's the way he is—and I don't want you to get hurt. He was asking a lot of questions about you even before you came down here.'

'Thanks, Rob, but I'm all grown up now,' she said with a smile. 'And I'm more than cautious where men are concerned. You don't need to worry about me.'

He reached for her arm and gave her a cautionary squeeze. 'Even so…you take care, Lacey. You're a gentle soul, and you've been through the mill lately. You deserve better.' His breathing became increasingly ragged, and Lacey saw that the heart monitor showed a rising, thundering rhythm.

'Perhaps you shouldn't talk any more,' she told him, getting to her feet. 'I'm going to give you an injection of something to slow your heart rate down, and then I'll go and organise the tests. The consultant will come along and see you once we have the results.'

'Okay.' Rob closed his eyes momentarily, clearly worn out by sharing those revelations with her.

Lacey went to prepare the injection, and once she had administered it she waited a while to gauge its effect. When Rob's heart and blood pressure rate began to drop, she felt able to leave him in the care of the nurse.

'I'll go and order an echocardiograph,' she told Emma. 'I've a feeling we might need to implant a device to regulate his heartbeat, so I'll ask the consultant to come and take a look at him.' She glanced at her watch. 'It's probably too late to bring him here now, but first thing in the morning would be good.'

Emma nodded. 'I'll take care of him in the meantime. Any changes and I'll let you know.'

'Thanks, Emma.'

Lacey wrote up a form for the technician and made arrangements for Rob to undergo the testing of his heart activity. Only when all those wheels were in motion did she stop and give some thought to what she had learned about her new neighbour.

No wonder Rob had his reservations about Jake. Rob had no time for the 'idle rich', as he called them, but Lacey's curiosity had been piqued.

Was Jake just out for a good time, taking life as he found it, and living it to the hilt?

And why did it bother her so much to think that a man with such charisma might be just an empty shell?

CHAPTER THREE

LACEY stretched, trying to ease away the stiffness in her shoulders. Now that her first shift at the hospital had come to an end and she parked her car in the garage, she was left with mixed feelings about the experience. It had been an eventful day, overall, and perhaps not quite what she had expected.

Meeting so many new colleagues had been a good thing. She had even managed to overcome the difficulties of working for a medical service that was different from anything she had known back home… But coming across one of her dearest friends lying ill in a hospital bed had been a huge shock.

That was the worst part of the day, the one that left her troubled and out of sorts, so that by now the muscles in her neck were knotted with tension.

She slid out of the car and went towards the front of the house. Darkness had fallen some time ago, and in the distance she could see that Jake's house was ablaze with light—it was coming from the windows, the open doors, and even the patio areas were bathed in gold. Soft music floated on the air, a lilting Caribbean rhythm, and it sounded as though the music was live, coming from an authentic steel band. She heard the occasional burst of laughter—obviously his party was in full swing.

She didn't stop to listen for long, though. More than anything, she needed to unwind, and perhaps the best way to do that would be to soak in a scented bath for a while, and let the warm water soothe her aching body.

She went upstairs, ran the water into the tub and added a silky essence that produced a satisfying blanket of foam.

When she came out of the bathroom some half

an hour later, she felt much more refreshed. She had put on soft cotton shorts and teamed them with a loose, button-through shirt that skimmed her hips and floated somewhere around mid-thigh. It wasn't exactly nightwear, but the material was soft and comfortable and it felt good next to her skin.

The music was still drifting on the night air, and she wandered restlessly about the kitchen. What was going on at Jake's house—what were his friends like? Was there some woman there who was particularly close to him? She cut that thought off at the root. She didn't care what Jake was up to...not really... It was just that her restless mind was busy mulling things over.

The night was still warm, and even though she was tired, she knew she wouldn't sleep. Instead, she poured herself a long glass of iced juice and wandered out to the dock area at the front of the house. It always calmed her to lean on the rail and look down at the water.

A few minutes later, she was disturbed by

a soft footfall, the faintest rasp of leather on paving, and a shadow loomed beside her. 'You look sad,' Jake murmured, coming to join her at the rail.

'Oh!' Lacey jumped. Where had he come from? He had appeared like a phantom out of nowhere. The iced clinked in her glass and she spilled some of the contents over the deck rail. She stared at him open-mouthed. 'That's the second time you've done that to me,' she said crossly. 'You have to stop sneaking up on me that way. One of these days you could give me a heart attack.'

'Nah—you're way too young for that,' he said, giving her an apologetic but altogether insincere smile. 'I didn't mean to startle you, though. As to sneaking…I'm pleading not guilty. I saw you out on the dock and decided to pay you a visit. I walked along the path in full view of anyone who cared to look, but you were so deep in thought you obviously didn't notice me.' He studied her reaction. 'Perhaps next time I'll hum a few lines of, "Hey-ho, here I come again".'

She tried to glower at him, but his resolute cheerfulness had the better of her, and she grudgingly gave in, her face relaxing a fraction. 'A warning would be great,' she agreed, 'but you really don't have to sing. I'm not sure I'm ready for that.'

He chuckled. 'It sounds as though you're not in the best of moods.' Sobering, he asked, 'So how did your day go? Was it tough? We all know the emergency room can be hell on earth at times… and that's not only as far as the patients are concerned.'

'That's true,' she acknowledged, 'but it wasn't like that for me today. Everyone was doing their best to make me feel at home, and that helped to make it a really good experience. It's just that I discovered what had happened to Rob—the reason why he didn't come home. He was admitted to hospital earlier today.'

Jake frowned, leaning against the rail beside her. 'I'm sorry to hear that. What happened?'

She told him the story, adding, 'I spoke to the consultant briefly, and he said that he'll come and have a look at him tomorrow and review all the tests. Because Rob has had several instances of collapse, he's thinking of implanting a monitoring device in his chest. It's very new technology—wireless, so that the consultant knows what's going on with his heart at any time and can use the information downloaded to his computer system to diagnose what exactly is causing the problem. If the patient starts to show dangerous symptoms the monitoring device will alert him and allow him to start or change treatment accordingly.'

Jake gave her a thoughtful look. 'It seems that everything possible is being done for him. Doesn't that make you feel any better?'

'I suppose it should.' Her mouth turned down at the corners. 'It's just that I'm not used to seeing Rob helpless like that. He's always been an outdoors kind of man, for ever on the move, wanting to keep busy and get the most out of life.'

Jake draped an arm lightly around her shoulders in a gesture of sympathy. 'I'm sure he's in good hands. They have an excellent treatment record at Bay View, and the consultant will do everything that's necessary to turn his condition around.'

'I know.' The words came out in a muffled tone. She was conscious of the heat from his arm gently seeping into her, and as he moved closer, she felt the brush of his long body next to hers. It was a good feeling, that warmth of human contact, and it occurred to her that it had been a long time since she had known such tenderness. She had a strange yearning to lean against him, to have him hold her and comfort her, but that would never do, would it?

This was Jake, a man she had known for barely two weeks, and instinct told her that she ought to be keeping him at arm's length. It was a pity her heart wasn't listening. Instead, it was beating out its own erratic rhythm, and seemed to be recklessly bent on overriding common sense.

A soft breeze stirred the air, and she looked out over the water. Moonlight glittered on its surface, beautiful in its serenity.

'Are you cold?' Jake asked, and she was suddenly reminded that they were standing out here on the dock, with her wearing little more than a cotton shift.

She shook her head. 'No, but I should go and put something on—a robe, or something.'

His mouth curved. 'You don't need to do that on my account. I'm perfectly happy for you to stay as you are… You feel very soft and cuddlesome to me, and you look like an angel, a dazzling, white angel who makes the moonbeams dance on the water.' His eyes gleamed in the darkness. 'Which reminds me…I came here to ask if you would come and join the party… There's dancing, friendly people, and lots of good food and drink to warm your soul.' He looked at her intently. 'What do you say? Will you come?'

She shook her head. 'I can't. It's late… I'm not dressed.'

'Late doesn't matter, does it? After all, you don't have to be at work till lunchtime tomorrow, do you? You said you were on the late shift all week. And as to being dressed, much as it goes against the grain to suggest altering what's perfect already, we could soon rectify that, couldn't we?'

He started to turn her around, and began to walk her towards the house. 'It really doesn't matter what you wear. You'll look gorgeous in anything, so choose whatever takes your fancy—maybe something cool and partyish.'

'I haven't said I'll come to your party,' she objected huskily as he urged her into the house, his arm still draped around her shoulders.

'Then I'll stay here with you and abandon my guests for even longer than I have done already. It will be all your fault when they say I'm a bad host.'

She gave him a look from under her lashes. 'Am I supposed to worry about that? Your problem is, you haven't learned to take no for an answer.'

He nodded. 'You're absolutely right.' He halted at the foot of the stairs, leaning negligently against the newel post. 'So what's it to be? Am I staying the night?' He paused, reflecting on that for a while. 'Actually, come to think of it, it seems to me that's much the better option.' Flame darted wickedly in his eyes.

'Oh, you're impossible.' She turned away from him and started up the stairs, but then she swivelled around and held out a forbidding hand as he made to follow her. 'You stay there,' she told him.

'Are you sure?' He gave her an innocent, wide-eyed look. 'I thought you might need some help deciding what to wear.'

'I'm *quite* sure.' Her blue eyes sparked a warning, and this time he paid heed, holding up his hands in mock submission.

'Okay, okay. I get the message.'

'That's good.'

Lacey started to climb the stairs once more, but in the background she heard his plaintive voice muttering, 'She doesn't like me a bit… She doesn't trust me…yet here I am, innocent as the day…'

'Innocent as an alligator on the prowl,' she retorted without looking back, and was rewarded with a soft splutter of laughter.

She dressed quickly in a simple, pencil-line dress made of a soft jersey fabric that clung to her figure like a second skin. She felt good in this dress. In delicate shades of blue, it enhanced the colour of her eyes, and lent her confidence. It had a V neckline and was waist cinching, and the bodice was embellished with a smattering of sparkling diamanté.

When she went back downstairs just a few minutes later, she found Jake was waiting for her in the hall. As she approached, he simply stared at her, an arrested look in his eyes, as though he couldn't believe what he was seeing. He gave a soft gasp of appreciation.

'You look fantastic,' he said, his gaze drifting over her. 'Like the girl of my dreams… I want to scoop you up and keep you all to myself.'

'Sorry. That's not an option.' She smiled. 'Besides, you said yourself that your guests will be wondering what's happened to you.'

'Maybe…but I left the caterers in charge. They'll see to it that no one goes hungry or without a drink.' He was still gazing at her in an enthralled fashion. 'Perhaps the party was a bad idea. It would be so much easier to get to know you better if we were to stay here.'

'On your way, neighbour,' she told him in a firm voice. 'You railroaded me into this, and you promised me food and drink… Besides, I have to confess I'm dying to see what your house is like inside. What I've seen from a distance looks magnificent, like a millionaire's retreat… all those different elevations and those land-scaped acres. Even the pale sunshine colouring looks good, with the white deck rails and tiled roofs and awnings. I'm intrigued to know what the rest of it looks like.'

'Then it will be my pleasure to show it to you,' he said. 'Though I don't think you need to feel envious in any way. The place you have here is just lovely—a lot smaller than mine, I grant you, but perfect for a couple, maybe, with a small family.'

He sent her a glance as they left the house and started out along the dock. 'Have you thought about selling up and finding yourself another place nearer to the hospital, or closer to your sister? I mean, you have no real reason to stay on here, do you? And Rob said you were hoping to meet up with your sister again soon.'

Her brow knotted. 'No, I hadn't thought about it at all. I'm still coming to terms with the move out here, and this was the natural choice of where to stay.'

He nodded. 'I can see how you would need time to acclimatise yourself. But if you ever do decide you want to sell up, I would give you a good price for the property.'

She looked at him in astonishment. 'Why on earth would you want to buy the place? Don't you have enough room to rattle about in already?'

He smiled. 'It's more about the land… I'd like to extend the dock, and build a marine basin… And then there's the orange grove at the back of the property. I already grow oranges, limes and grapefruit, but with your land added to mine I could do it on a commercial basis. There's always a market for fresh fruit or fruit juices.'

They were approaching his property by now, and she frowned, studying him briefly in the glow of lanterns that were sited at strategic intervals all around. 'I think you'll have to look elsewhere for any business opportunities,' she told him. 'I have good memories of the house from when it was a family home, and I don't believe I'm ready to sell up. I'm just getting used to being here, and the familiarity helps.'

He nodded, but his eyes had darkened a fraction as though he was disappointed by her response. 'Well, the offer will still be there if you change your mind.'

He ushered her along the sweeping, wide drive that led up to his house. The gardens were beautifully landscaped, with palm trees making striking silhouettes against the skyline. Bougainvillea shrubs provided glorious splashes of colour along the curving borders, their heart-shaped leaves and flowers enclosed by scarlet bracts. Oleander vied for room with a variety of herbaceous plants, the dark green leaves a rich contrast to its delicate yellow and white flowers. Here and there she saw breathtaking clusters of orchids peeping through the display, and above all there was the delicate perfume of frangipani, filling her senses with all that was tropical and exotic.

'I'll fix you a drink and then introduce you to some of the people here,' Jake murmured, his hand resting lightly on the small of her back.

'Mostly they're friends, or business acquaint-
ances of my father, and some are people I know
from Miami. I think you'll like them.'

He showed her the bar, set up in a corner of
the terrace, where a waiter was mixing cocktails
for anyone who cared to try them. 'How about
a Florida Sunrise?' Jake suggested.

'I don't think I've ever tried one,' Lacey said.
'What is it?'

'It's delicious… It's made by pouring a dash
of grenadine into the bottom of a glass—that's
a syrup made from red currants and pome-
granates—then you add crushed ice, pour in
Bacardi rum and top up with orange juice. I
think you'll like it.'

'Sounds good to me,' she agreed, and when
she sipped her drink a moment later she was
pleasantly surprised. 'This is really great.'

He smiled. 'Trust me,' he said. 'I won't steer
you wrong.'

She looked into his eyes and wondered if that
could be true. She simply couldn't work him

out. In truth, she might be here in body and spirit, but her mind was still trying to fathom his surprise offer to buy her house. Rob had been right when he'd said that Jake was eccentric. You never knew what to expect from him.

He introduced her around, as promised, but did it en route as they explored the house. Everyone was friendly, intent on having a good time, and after a while Lacey began to relax.

She was fascinated by this glimpse into the way he lived. The kitchen was superb, richly fitted out with warm-coloured mahogany cupboards and wall units, mostly glass fronted, and the whole was finished with gleaming granite worktops. There were built-in ovens and appliances made from stainless steel and dark glass, and at one end of the room there was a corner sink unit. The opposite corner was made up of a wall of glass, looking out onto a covered deck, which in turn overlooked the sea.

'Help yourself to something to eat,' Jake told her. 'The least I can do is feed you up after you've been hard at work all day. Besides, I owe you for the empanadas.'

'Thanks.' Her glance swept over the feast that had been laid out on a large island unit to one side of the kitchen. 'But they fade into insignificance next to this. It all looks mouth-wateringly delicious.'

Among the treats on offer, there were dishes of fresh pink shrimp set out on beds of lettuce leaves, plates of rye bread garnished with pastrami, cheese and sauerkraut, and laced with salad dressing, and there were crispy tortilla chips topped with guacamole, sour cream, salsa and cheese.

'Try a bit of everything,' he suggested, handing her a plate.

'Okay.' She tasted several of the gourmet dishes on offer, savouring the different flavours and textures, and then when she felt she could eat no more, she glanced around. She was captivated by the understated opulence of his home. It was set out in open-plan fashion, the different areas marked out by a change in floor covering—ceramic tiles in the kitchen, and oak boards in the living and dining room areas. There were wide archways leading from one room to another, and the whole gave a feeling of spaciousness and light.

'If you've finished eating for the moment,' he said as she put aside her plate, 'I'll give you a tour of the rest of the house.'

'Thanks, I'd like that. What I've seen so far is way beyond my expectations.' The furniture was upholstered in pale, luxurious fabrics, with scatter cushions adding a dash of colour here and there. Simple flower arrangements and the greenery of ferns made everything complete. 'You have a lovely home.' Home was the operative word. Somehow the elegance and luxury faded into the background, with the overall feeling that this was not just a beautifully furnished house. It was a place where you could live and relax and be yourself.

His smile was warm. 'I'm glad you like it.'

She nodded, but inside she was asking herself why on earth he would want to have her house as well as this one. His talk of extending the dock and fruit groves somehow didn't ring true. 'Let me show you around upstairs,' he murmured, placing a hand beneath her elbow and leading her through the crowded rooms to the stairs. 'There are five bedrooms in all,' he added, as they made their way to the second floor, 'and they've all been sited to look out over the sea.'

He pushed open a door. 'This is the master suite. It's the biggest room, and has a deck area, so first thing in the morning I can go out there and breathe in the fresh air.'

'I know that feeling. It's lovely to be able to do that.' She could imagine him standing out here in the early morning, half-awake, bare-chested as the sun rose and cast its glow over his golden skin, his long body lithe and tautly muscled.

'Yes, it is.' He glanced at her. 'Are you all right? You look very pensive all of a sudden.'

She blinked, and gave him a startled look.

What was the matter with her? Heat rushed through her body in a swift wave, going straight to her head. For a moment there she had drifted off into a reverie of intoxicating dreams and wild imaginings. 'Um…I'm fine.' She tried to rally her thoughts. 'There must have been more rum than orange juice in that Florida Sunrise.'

He laughed. 'The night's young. When the food you've eaten begins to take effect, I'm sure you could risk another one.'

She wasn't so sure that it was the drink that was affecting her. The plain truth was she couldn't think straight when he was close by. He had a strange effect on her nervous system, and by now she ought to know better than to let him get under her guard.

'Bathrooms,' he said, steering her out of the danger area. 'There are several, but they're all pretty much alike.' He opened a door that led off from the main bedroom. 'This is my en suite… it's lovely and cool at the height of the summer.

You can just lean against those marble walls and let the heat drizzle out of you.'

She tried it, leaning back against the cool tiles and waiting for the heat to dissipate. Only it didn't happen, because Jake was standing in front of her and all at once his arms were gliding around her waist, and his long body was lightly pressuring hers.

She half closed her eyes, and when his lips brushed hers it was everything that she had dreamed of…exhilarating, intoxicating, a ripple of pleasure that started with her lips and flowed from there through every particle of her being. His hands gently caressed the curve of her hips, drawing her towards him, and a pool of heat started to grow inside her, eddying out in circles of exquisite delight.

She wasn't in control of herself any more. His hands roamed lightly over her body, and she realised he was playing her like a finely tuned instrument, stroking every quivering nerve fibre as though he knew exactly how to coax the response he wanted.

She moved against him, loving the way their bodies fitted, his hard, muscled torso against her soft, feminine curves. He groaned raggedly, deepening the kiss, and then let his lips trail over her hot skin, swooping downwards, exploring the smooth curve of her breasts.

A soft gasp escaped her. Her mind was whirling, and she was overwhelmed by these new, unbidden sensations that rocketed through her body. Why was this happening? How was he able to do this to her...how was he able to make her feel this way?

This was something she had never experienced before...not even with Nick, who had been everything to her at one time, until it had all gone wrong. Why would she even think of allowing herself to fall into that same situation all over again?

She laid her hands flatly on Jake's chest, and even that had the effect of making her weak with desire. Her fingertips moved shakily along the line of his rib cage. Why was she letting this happen?

'Jake,' she managed at last, 'Jake, I can't do this. I don't know what I was thinking. I'm not ready for this.'

'You're delicious, you're beautiful,' he murmured huskily against the smooth velvet of her throat, as though he hadn't heard her. 'You're everything I could ever want.'

She tried to draw back from him, and a faint groan rumbled in his throat, the flat of his hands supporting her spine, resisting her efforts. 'What could be wrong about this? I know you want me,' he whispered. 'You melted in my arms, you kissed me, you showed me how much you wanted me.'

'Jake, no… I mean it. I'm sorry.' Determined now, she pushed against his chest until he stopped caressing her, and his body became rigid with tension. 'I'm sorry,' she said again.

Slowly, reluctantly, he eased himself away

from her. 'You don't have anything to apologise for,' he said in a low, roughened tone. 'I should have known better. I invited you here and you should have been safe in my home, even from the likes of me.'

He straightened. 'Don't let it spoil your evening,' he said. 'Go back downstairs and join the others, if you will. I just need a minute or two to get myself together.'

She looked at him and saw the lines of tension in his face. She daren't do anything other than he suggested. It was clear to see that he was struggling in the aftermath of their passionate encounter, and she didn't want to risk any repercussions by staying on.

She left him there, and went to join the rest of his guests. Perhaps she would be able to slip quietly away.

CHAPTER FOUR

SLIPPING away from the party wasn't going to be quite as easy as she had imagined, Lacey discovered when she walked out onto the deck outside Jake's sitting room. Her plan was to follow the path of the deck around the house to the nearest exit and then flee into the darkness.

Instead, she was waylaid by one of the male guests. 'Hi,' he said, coming to stand beside her. 'I'm Ben.'

'Hello, Ben.' She gave him a brief nod, a wave of frustration washing over her as her escape route was effectively cut off. He was around Jake's age, fair haired, good-looking, and with an athletic build.

'You seem to be all alone,' he murmured, 'and without a drink. We can't have that. Have you tried one of our Rum Runner cocktails?'

'Um, no, I haven't.' Lacey frowned, trying to work out an alternative getaway strategy. Would she do better to wind her way through the crowded living room, or would that attract even more attention?

'We can soon remedy that.' Ben's hand slid beneath her elbow and he began to gently turn her in the direction of the bar.

'Well, actually, I was thinking of leaving...' Lacey started to turn away. 'I only planned on dropping by for an hour or so.'

Ben lightly sucked in his breath. 'I doubt Jake would forgive me if I let you slip away without him being able to see you to your door. You're his neighbour, aren't you? I overheard him introducing you to people when I was over by the bar. Besides, you can't think of leaving until you've let me get you a drink.' He laid a hand lightly in the small of her back.

'What's going on here, Ben?' Jake asked, his tone dry as he walked through the open glass doors and came towards them. 'Are you making a play for my girl? I might have known you wouldn't be able to resist the temptation. I can't leave you alone for five minutes.'

Lacey caught her breath. *My girl?* It was difficult enough for her to get herself back on an even keel without him saying things like that. And she certainly hadn't expected to see him again this evening. Her retreat had been in motion and now all her plans were shot to pieces, thanks to Ben's intervention.

As for Jake, he seemed to be back to his normal self and he wasn't giving a hint as to what had gone on between them either by look or gesture.

The two men eyed each other like friendly adversaries, and she guessed each of them was well aware of the other's thoughts and likely moves.

'Make a play for her? As if I would do that,' Ben retorted with a crooked smile. 'I was just persuading her to try one of the smugglers' specials. After all, we can't have a celebration of our activities without drinking to the felons who used to live on the Keys and ply their illegal trade, can we?'

Lacey's eyes widened a little, and Jake commented lightly, 'See what you've done now, Ben? Her mind's ticking over and she's beginning to think we're involved in all sorts of nefarious activities.'

'Ah, well, there's the thing...' Ben gave a wicked grin. 'I always felt there was a dangerous excitement in diving for treasure. It kind of gets the blood racing, don't you think?'

'It's certainly dangerous.' Jake's comment was softly spoken, his blue-grey gaze overcast as a shadow flitted over his usually cheerful expression. Lacey looked from one to the other in bewilderment.

'I'm lost,' she said, all thoughts of escape driven from her mind. 'What are you both talking about?'

'Come and try a Rum Runner and I'll explain,'

Jake murmured, shaking off his introspection and ushering her towards the bar.

The bartender mixed the drink, adding ice to a glass, then pouring over it equal measures of pineapple and orange juice, blackberry liqueur, banana liqueur and topping that with a generous measure of rum. Finally, he added a splash of grenadine and a slice of orange.

Jake handed Lacey the long glass, inviting her to taste the mixture. 'This goes way back to the days of prohibition,' he murmured, 'when smugglers used to bring in beer and rum from Cuba to the Keys and stash it away in basement hiding places. Of course, your people, the British, weren't entirely innocent in all this… They helped us out by sending along their own contributions—whisky, rye and Scotch.'

'I'm not having this slurring of my good name,' she said, raising a brow. 'That was way before my time, and I'm sure we'd never do such a thing now.' She sent him a mischievous look from under her lashes. 'Mind you, seeing all this wealth and opulence around me, I expect you'd have a hard time denying that your ancestors were involved in some way.'

He let that ride, his mouth making a rueful twist, while Lacey sipped her drink. It was deliciously fruity, and it packed quite a punch. Heat pooled in her abdomen and spread slowly throughout her body. 'Whoo-hoo…' she said. 'I can see why these are popular.'

Jake laughed. 'They're especially good if you don't have to drive home.'

'Or dive in the morning,' Ben put in. 'I'm thinking I shall have to put it off until the weekend.'

Lacey frowned. 'So you weren't kidding when you mentioned diving for treasure? What's that all about?'

'You don't know?' Ben looked surprised. 'I imagined Jake must have told you all about it. That's partly why he holds these get-togethers, to raise money for the diving expeditions…or at least, that's the reason for some of the parties. People sign up for shares in the company.'

'Company?' She shook her head. 'I'm still confused. Are you saying that you dive for treasure and get to keep the proceeds? What treasure?'

'The Keys are renowned for the number of ships that foundered in the waters around here,' Jake explained. 'Especially Spanish galleons from the sixteenth century onwards. They sank because they were caught up in hurricanes, or were dashed against the coral reefs, or maybe simply because their captains were unaware how treacherous the waters could be around here.'

'And many of the ships carried hoards of silver and gold—and sank to the bottom of the sea,' Ben tacked on. 'Which is where Jake's grandfather found his fortune. He spent years searching for wrecks, and eventually his hard work paid off.'

'Of course, the treasure is all classed as belonging to the state these days,' Jake said, 'so you need permits for everything, and the state decides what you can keep.'

'Except that Jake's grandfather established his claim before it became law,' Ben explained, 'and he secured all the rights to his find. So he established a company, and now the company's divers search the wreck site and take shares in any finds they make. Of course, there will always be those people who don't like to take the legal route. They'll dive without permits and try to smuggle out anything they find. Some of the hoards are worth a small fortune.'

Lacey stared at Jake. 'I'm lost for words,' she said. No wonder he had that wicked, devilish streak about him. It went back to the days of rumrunners and treasure hunters and ran through his blood like a rich, red wine.

'So, do you dive at the sites of the wrecks?' she asked him. 'Is that why I see you going out in the boats most days?'

He shook his head. 'I used to.' His features tightened momentarily, but then he recovered himself and added, 'Nowadays I prefer to go out and do a bit of fishing, or sometimes I'll scubadive simply for pleasure. Have you ever tried it?'

She nodded. 'I have…when I've been on holiday sometimes, but never actually around here.'

'Then you must let me take you. The underwater coral reefs here are beautiful and not to be missed.'

Lacey frowned. The casual invitation had caught her completely unawares. Was he trying to change the subject and divert attention from the treasure seeking?

His gaze skimmed over her as she sipped her drink. 'How about we make a trip out there on Saturday? I'll pick you up and we'll try out my new boat.'

'It's finished?' Her eyes widened. 'You must have put some hours in to manage that.'

'Yes, I have.' He smiled. 'So, do we have a date?'

She shook her head. After the way she had fallen for temptation earlier, it would be sheer folly to ask for more of the same, wouldn't it? It would just prove that she had no common sense, and that she'd learned nothing from her break-up with Nick. Wasn't Nick the same sort of pleasure-loving individual as Jake? They were two of a kind, and she wasn't about to make the same mistake twice. 'Sorry, but it's no deal.' She sent him a penetrating glance. 'Anyway, unlike some, I have a job to go to, and I'll be working on Saturday. That's my shift for the week, Tuesday to Saturday.'

It was Jake's turn to raise his brows. 'Did I hear a criticism somewhere in there? Perhaps you don't think I earn my keep?'

'It wasn't a criticism, just an observation.'

His gaze narrowed on her. 'I have a notion it was a little more than that. Do you think there's something wrong in treasure hunting?'

'Not at all. I think you're very lucky to have

the opportunity to do it and succeed at the same time.'

'But you're sceptical. I can see it in your eyes.'

She wriggled her shoulders uncomfortably. 'I'm sure it's very exciting, and nice work for some, but it's not what you might call a regular job, is it?' She paused. 'I know that exploring wrecks can be difficult and hazardous, and the rewards are probably tremendous, but I'm not convinced it's what you call real work.'

She glanced at Ben. 'Sorry, Ben. I'm not having a go at you…but I can't imagine that exploring a wreck in the hope of finding treasure is going to provide anyone with a bread-and-butter income.'

Ben smiled crookedly. 'You're right. It wouldn't do to rely on it, but when we do occasionally locate another piece of a hoard on the seabed, we find it's a very lucrative business. The rest of the time, I work from nine to five as the director of a distributing company. So, you see, I do have my feet firmly on the ground.'

'Stop trying to impress the girl,' Jake intervened dryly, his eyes narrowing on his friend. 'I saw her first.'

'That doesn't mean she's falling head over heels for you,' Ben retorted. 'She turned you down for the scubadive, remember.'

'Okay, okay…the pair of you can stop squabbling,' Lacey put in. 'I'm going home…to sleep and get ready for another day in Emergency. You can both stay and party your hearts out.' Her mouth curved. 'It has been lovely seeing around your house, Jake, and meeting your friends. Thanks for bringing me along, but I really do have to go now.'

'I'll walk you home,' he said, and as Ben made a move to go with them he threw him a hard look that said, *Back off.*

Ben took it in good part, inclining his head towards Lacey. 'Bye, Lacey,' he said. 'I hope I see you again soon.'

'Me, too,' she said.

'Not if I have anything to do with it,' Jake muttered under his breath. He wrapped a possessive arm around Lacey and went with her to the door.

'You really don't have to see me home,' she murmured. 'I'll be fine.'

'Even so…I'll walk with you.' He sent her a sideways glance as they walked out on to the terrace and headed for the path. 'You seem to be quite concerned about my laid-back lifestyle. I do have to work on company business from time to time, you know?'

'Yes, so Rob told me.'

'Hmm. I guessed you might have been talking to him. I think it bothers him that I don't have a nine-to-five job. It's unfortunate, but Rob and I never quite got along, for some reason, and I suspect that's at the root of it. I used to invite him over to the house, but he wouldn't take me up on any of my offers. I had the feeling he'd written me off as some kind of rich party boy.'

'It's possible you may be right there.' She glanced at him. She would have liked to ask him how he came to spend his days doing little of any importance, but the answer might disturb her too much. He might tell her he preferred things that way...and if he wanted her to know more, he would tell her, wouldn't he?

'Seriously, though,' she added, 'Rob is a very private person, and it can be difficult to get to know him. I think that's why he preferred to live out here in relative isolation. It's only now that I've decided to come and live here that he's had to think through his options, and he decided to move nearer to his family. I think the move will do him good.' She frowned. 'Of course, he'll have to wait awhile to do that, now that he's to be fitted with an implant. He'll probably stay in the area until his medical problems have been sorted out. In fact, he'll probably come back to stay at my place for a short time. He left quite a few of his belongings with me.'

'I expect he'll be glad to do that.'

By now they had reached her house and she halted by the door, hesitating a moment as she thought over the night's events. She was drawn to Jake in more ways than she cared to imagine, but he was a definite threat to her peace of mind. He wasn't like other men. There was something about him that set off warning bells in her head every time he was near. And tonight had been no exception. He had plied her with food and drink until the world had taken on a rosy glow, and maybe that was why he had managed to slip through the cracks in her defences.

'I'll say goodnight, then,' she murmured. 'Thanks for showing me around your house, and for walking me home.'

'You're very welcome…any time.' He moved closer to her, his voice a husky drawl. 'If there's anything you want…help of some sort, a friendly chat…*me*…you only have to call and I'll be there in a second.' Flame darted in his eyes as his glance trailed over her, and an imp of a smile tugged at the corners of his mouth.

A pulse started to beat heavily in her throat, and her whole body filled with heat. 'I'll bear it in mind,' she said in a rough-edged voice, evading him as he sought to move closer. She turned her key in the lock. 'Bye, Jake.'

'Bye.' He left her, turning to walk back along the wharf, and only then did she begin to relax. She would try to put him out of her mind. A good night's sleep was what she needed, and then maybe she could concentrate on what she knew to be safe—the tried-and-tested route of focussing on her work, or the diversion of getting in touch with friends and family.

At least work would keep her busy and her mind occupied, and, sure enough, next day, at the hospital, it was as though the party had taken place a lifetime ago. There was no time here for reflection.

She spent a couple of hours in the emergency room, treating people with breathing difficulties and various fractures, and then when there was a bit of a lull she went to find out how Rob was doing.

'I'm feeling much better now that the medication has kicked in,' he told her. 'The consultant said he'll do the implant later this morning.'

'I'm sure you'll be fine,' Lacey reassured him. 'Once it's in place, we can monitor what's going on with your heart, and think about different ways to treat you. From the look of the ECG recordings, the electrical system that regulates your heartbeat has gone awry, and we need to find out which particular part is causing the problem.'

Rob smiled wearily. 'It all sounds very complicated to me, but I trust you. I know you're doing your best for me, and I'll go along with whatever the consultant suggests.'

'That's good.' She smiled at him. 'I'll come and see you when it's over. In the meantime,

I think your parents and your brother are on their way to see you. Emma said she saw them coming from the restaurant.'

'Yeah, it was good of them to come check up on me.' He studied her thoughtfully. 'How about you? Have you heard from your sister Grace lately?'

Lacey nodded. 'She said she'll come over with the children some time next week…she's bringing the dog, too, rather than put him into kennels. Matt has to go away on business for a few days, but I'm sure he'll find time to visit. She even said they were thinking of relocating down here. Matt is setting up a new office in Key Largo, so they'll be much nearer to me…a straight drive along the highway and we can be together. I'm really looking forward to seeing them all again. It's not the same, talking on the phone.'

'No, it isn't. It can be frustrating when there are hundreds or thousands of miles between you, and the only link you have is email or a phone call.' He looked at her oddly, and she wondered what going through his mind. Was he thinking about their friendship?

Lacey frowned, not knowing what to say. She laid her hand on his and squeezed his fingers gently, an unspoken communication passing between them.

'I always had a soft spot for you,' he said quietly. 'Only you were hung up on Nick, and I knew I didn't stand a chance. And it's no better now that you and he are through, because he's made you cautious of any man who crosses your path.'

'Yes, that's true,' she admitted, 'but it goes deeper than that. I'm sorry, Rob…but you know, you and I will always have something special, a great friendship. I can't offer you anything more than that, because it's how I've always felt about you—that you're like my best friend, or a brother to me.'

He made a rueful face. 'I'd guessed as much. Besides, I knew I wouldn't get a look in when you moved into the house, not with Jake living next door. Women always seem to fall for him, and I get the feeling that I'm definitely out-classed. Knowing Jake, I'm pretty sure he's pulling out all the stops to get your attention. He is, isn't he?'

'What makes you think that?'

He made a grimace. 'It was easy enough to work it out. He sent me a fruit basket with a card saying he was sorry to hear that I was ill, and that he wished me well. I knew it must have been you who told him. It just confirmed what I thought… I knew from the outset that he would try to keep in fairly regular, close contact with you. He isn't one to let the grass grow under his feet, is he?'

'Well, no, you're right about that.' She looked briefly around the room until her glance came to rest on a wicker basket brimming with ripe, gloriously coloured fruits. 'It was thoughtful of him to send the fruit, though, wasn't it? You've all sorts there—oranges, mangoes, passion fruit, grapes. They look luscious.'

'Yes, it was a great gesture. Help yourself to anything you fancy.' He frowned, his mouth turning down at the corners. 'I suppose this means I'll have to be nice to him now…at least for a while.'

She laughed and ruffled his hair. 'You're such a grump, Rob. Think positive…when you're feeling better you can hightail it out of here, without looking back. Then he won't be a problem to you.'

'Maybe.'

She left him to rest before his family arrived to visit, and went back to work. Emma prepared a suture trolley so that Lacey could treat a man who had gashed his arm in a surfing accident.

'That's quite a gash you have there, Sam,' Emma commented. 'Still, it's clean and straight, so it should heal nicely once it has been stitched.'

'You'll have to stay out of the water for a

while, though,' Lacey warned him as she applied the sutures. 'You don't want it to become infected.'

He nodded. 'I suppose I'll have to make do with sitting around the poolside instead.' He smiled. 'Do you do any surfing, or watersports of any kind?'

'I've never tried out a surfboard. I don't think I'd have the balance,' she answered, putting the last stitch in place. 'I'll prescribe some antibiotics, just to be on the safe side.'

'What about you?' Sam turned his head to glance at Emma, who was jotting down notes in his file. 'Do you go in for watersports?'

'I enjoy snorkelling,' Emma said. 'But scuba-diving's the best, for me. You can go deeper and get a closer look at the coral reefs. What I really want next is an underwater camera so that I can take pictures.'

'I have a camera. Maybe we could go together some time?' he suggested. 'Unless you're already dating someone?'

Emma's cheeks were flushed. Clearly, she hadn't been expecting such a direct invitation. 'Well, uh…no, but I…uh…' She sent him a cautious glance. 'Um…I'll think about it.'

'Good. That's a start, anyway.' He looked pleased with himself, and Lacey decided it was time to remove herself from the treatment room and leave the two of them together. Emma would put a dressing on the wound and clear away the suture equipment so that Lacey was free to attend other patients.

'Just make sure you keep that wound dry until the stitches have been removed,' she reminded Sam.

'I will.'

The rest of her shift passed quickly. They were inundated with people bearing all kinds of wounds and ailments, but Lacey was glad of the diversion. Otherwise Jake would have intruded on her thoughts far more than she would have liked.

As it was, he was waiting for her when she

returned home later that night. Or, at least, he was stacking the lobster pots along the wharf, and paused to come over and talk to her after she had parked her car.

'How did it go?' he asked. 'Is there any news of Rob?'

She nodded. 'The implant was a success…it's working fine, and he's feeling much better now that the medication has started to calm his heart down.' She smiled. 'He says thanks for the fruit basket. It was a lovely gesture on your part.'

Jake shrugged, and she couldn't help noticing the way his powerful biceps strained against the material of his navy coloured T-shirt. 'It was the least I could do. We may not get along too well, but that doesn't mean I don't sympathise with his predicament.'

She glanced towards the lobster pots. 'Do you manage to trap any?'

He nodded. 'Enough to send off to the local store and restaurant.' He looked at her, but his features were shadowed in the darkness. 'I'd still like the chance to take you out in my boat. You'd be its very first passenger, and maybe I could convince you that sailing and scubadiving around here is fun. We could head out to the reefs on Sunday, if you like.'

She pressed her lips together, looking doubtful. 'I don't know… I'm very busy, with the new job, and small decorating jobs around the house.'

'Can't I persuade you?' His voice dropped into a low, coaxing tone. 'I'm sure you would love it…and you know what they say about all work and no play…'

'I'm not going to let that worry me,' she said lightly. 'I'm perfectly happy as I am. And as to going anywhere with you, I have to tell you I've been warned to be on my guard.'

'I can guess who was the one giving the warning.' He made a wry face. 'Seriously, if I promise to be on my best behaviour, would you reconsider? I know where the best reefs are, and it would be an experience to remember, I'm sure.'

She gave it some thought. Where was the harm

after all? Hadn't he been considerate enough to think of Rob when he was ill in hospital?

'Well, maybe I'll give it a try.' The words were out before she had a chance to stop them, and he swooped on her, giving her a hug.

'That's my girl.' He was smiling as he looked down into her eyes. 'I'll come and fetch you bright and early on Sunday morning. You won't regret it, I promise.'

'Well, I dare say we'll see about that,' Lacey murmured. Her mind was already clouding over with indecision, and being wrapped in his arms didn't help a bit. She wasn't at all sure she was doing the right thing, and by agreeing to go along with him she was probably setting herself up for trouble. He was a pirate by nature, a devil of the high seas, a man who lived life by his own rules.

It was too late to take it back, though. Jake released her, and was already striding back along the dock towards his house, whistling a cheerful tune, his step jaunty.

CHAPTER FIVE

'I'M ASSUMING the water will be warm enough
so that I won't need a wetsuit,' Lacey said, when
Jake came to call for her on Sunday morning.
She was wearing a T-shirt and shorts over her
swimsuit, and with the sun shining over everyone and everything it was an easy bet that she
would dry out soon enough when she came out
of the water.

'Yes, you can rely on it. In fact, you could
swim naked if you wanted.' He sent her a hopeful look, but she fixed him with a glittering blue
gaze.

'I don't think so.'

'No?'

'Definitely not.'

'Oh, well,' he sighed. 'I suppose it was worth a
try...' He grinned. 'But as to water temperature,

that's the beauty of a tropical climate…life just gets better and better. In fact, when you think about it, everything in the Keys is hassle free, laid back, and it's all about simply having fun.'

'I've noticed.'

'Well, we all succumb to the atmosphere in the end. They call it Keys disease, because it creeps up on you before you realise what's happened.'

She smiled. 'You *would* go along with that. You're a hedonist, through and through.'

He shrugged. 'The way I see it, life's too short to be working and worrying, if it's not necessary.' His glance moved over her. 'Today will be good for you. You need to loosen up a little.'

'Do I?' She raised a brow. 'You're beginning to sound like my ex-boyfriend. He thought life was all about having a good time, taking days off to laze in the sun with a cool drink by the lounger, or chill out in his apartment.'

'Are you saying you didn't go along with that?'

'Naturally I did, to some extent. Who wouldn't want to relax and enjoy life? But obviously we had different opinions as to the timing.' Her mouth turned down at the corners. 'That's partly why he's an ex.'

He gave a soft chuckle. 'So tell me about him. There must have been more to him than pure pursuit of pleasure, or I can't see you going with him in the first place. Didn't you want to pull up your lounger alongside him?'

'Of course, and I often did…but not when we had to study for specialist exams, or when I was expected to put in an appearance for an important tutorial. Anyway, it wasn't just about that.' She frowned. 'He started drinking heavily and I could see it was taking its toll on him. He didn't see that there was a problem, and if I said anything he made me feel as though I was a swot and a spoilsport, and it ruined everything between us.'

Her expression was sombre. 'I didn't want to pour cold water on his plans, but my career's important to me, and I wasn't happy to make do with second-class results. I don't think Nick ever really understood that.'

'Is that what he finished up with…second-class results? I'm assuming he's a doctor, like you?' He leaned against the nearby worktop, watching her as she gathered up various bits and pieces and added them to the holdall on the kitchen table.

She nodded. 'He had to do retakes, and managed to scrape by, but it was such a waste when he had the ability to do so much better.' She sighed. 'I suppose that didn't really matter, if he was happy with the way things were going. It was his choice, but I felt that he was sliding downhill, losing control, and I wanted to help him, but he wouldn't listen. He said some harsh things to me and made me feel that I was the one who was in the wrong, the one who needed to change. I suppose it was a defensive reaction on his part.'

'So you split up?'

'Yes, eventually. I felt guilty, because I could see him going off the rails, and I wanted to do more to get him back on track, but it became obvious I was wasting my time. He didn't want my help.'

She added a towel to the bag. 'I was going through my own problems, after losing my parents, and he wasn't there for me when I needed him. There should have been more understanding between us, of how we each felt as individuals, but when that was missing, we just began to realise that we were miles apart in our outlook on life. It was better to end it.'

She closed the zip on the holdall as though she was closing off that part of her life for ever. It hadn't felt that way at the time, but perhaps now that she could look back on it, she was relieved that it was over.

He frowned. 'Sometimes people have to discover for themselves that they're losing control. Until they do that, all their friends and relatives can do is pick up the pieces.'

'I suppose so.'

'What happened to your parents? Do you mind talking about it?'

She shook her head. 'It was a car accident. The only consolation was that it was all over very quickly for them. I don't think they knew what had hit them.'

'I'm sorry. That must have been hard...for you and for your sister.'

'Yes, it was.' She pressed her lips together. It wasn't a subject she wanted to dwell on. Besides, he must have gone through the same process of grief if both of his parents had passed on.

He picked up the holdall from the table. 'Is this what you're taking with you? Is it all packed and ready to go?'

'Yes. I've hunted out all my old scuba equipment, mask, fins and jacket, but I'm assuming you have the compressed air tanks?'

'That's right, I do. They're stowed away on board the boat, along with a picnic hamper so that we can have lunch. All you need to bring is yourself.'

Her mouth curved. 'Sounds good to me. And a picnic, too…that was a great piece of thinking. I wondered whether to bring along anything to eat, but then I decided we'd probably be able to pick up something if we tied up alongside a waterfront eating place, or some such.'

'We can still do that. The picnic is just to tide us over in case we get ravenous along the way.' His gaze wandered slowly over her shapely curves. 'Of course, there's hunger, and then there's hunger…'

Her brows lifted a fraction, her blue eyes sparking, so that he lifted his hands in submission and said quickly, 'Okay, I promise, I'm on my best behaviour. I'm an absolute saint.'

'Well, that's good to hear,' she countered, 'because I'm really looking forward to exploring these reefs, and the only reason I'm doing it is because you said I could trust you.'

He pulled a face. 'Life can be sheer torture sometimes.'

She laughed. 'Show me this boat, Jake. I can't wait to see how you've finished it off.'

'I think you'll like it.' He led the way to where the boat was moored by the dock, and Lacey stood for a moment, taking it in.

'It's beautiful,' she said, looking at it in awe. 'It looks so much bigger out here on the water, and I didn't realise there would be a cabin.' Perhaps the cabin section had been in another part of the barn, under wraps. 'This is a work of art,' she murmured. 'You must be really proud of what you've done.'

'I guess I am.' He smiled. 'There's a galley, with facilities for cooking—nothing grand, of course, given the space, but enough to heat a pan of something or boil water for coffee. And I've managed to fit in a small icebox. There are a couple of sleeping berths as well, in case they're needed.'

'It looks as though there's still room on deck

for the lobster pots, too.' Lacey was full of admiration for his handiwork. She couldn't take her eyes off it.

'We won't be needing those today.' He held out a hand to her. 'Let me help you aboard.' His fingers grasped hers, warm and strong as he steadied her. 'I thought of calling her *Lacey*, since your arrival here spurred me on to finish her quickly. What do you think?'

Her eyes widened. 'I think I'm honoured, but I'm not sure I deserve such a tribute.'

The boat was truly a work of craftsmanship. It was a small cruiser, fitted out with upholstered seats that converted to sleeping berths with storage compartments underneath. The galley was a masterpiece, with everything you would need for home comfort, a fridge, icebox and small cooker all neatly placed to make good use of available space, with a table alongside where you could sit and eat. There was even a cupboard for medical equipment, and a lock-up box for valuables. It was all finished to perfection.

Jake started up the motor, and it purred into action. Lacey stood beside him, looking out through the clear glass windows of the cabin, as he steered them out onto the open sea. The doors at the back of the cabin were open to allow the breeze to waft through, and there was a sun hatch that was open to assist with the airflow.

'I thought we'd head out to a reef some twenty miles away,' Jake said. 'It'll take us half an hour or so to get there, but I think it's well worth a visit. It's a place where a British ship ran aground back in the 1700s. All the crew survived and many of them made their way to the Bahamas, but the captain ordered the ship to be burned so that the enemy wouldn't be able to salvage anything at some time in the future. There's not a lot to see of the wreck these days, unless you know what you're looking for, but the anchor and chain are very clearly visible.'

'How deep will we be diving?'

'Around forty feet, so it's comfortable for someone who doesn't dive frequently. I'll show you the most interesting areas. It's one of the best reefs in the region.'

Some half an hour later, they arrived at their destination. Jake secured the boat to a mooring buoy and they both put on the scuba equipment and readied themselves for the dive. Other boats were moored nearby, so Lacey guessed this was a popular place.

'Are you ready?' Jake asked.

'Yes.'

'Okay, then. You probably know this already, but you must be careful not to get too close to the coral because some species have razor-sharp edges that can cut into your skin, even through a wetsuit…and others are soft and look like plants, but if you touch them they break off and die. Then there are the ones that sting…'

'I think I get the picture,' she said with a smile.

'Good.' He nodded. 'Look out for the fire coral, especially. It's called that because of the burning sensation it can cause if you happen to rub up against it. It's generally a beige colour with a hint of green, and it's a bit like a stalk with short branches.'

'Thanks for the warning. I'll be extra-careful.'

Finally, they were ready to go into the sea, and when she slid into the water she found it was warm, like silk, on her body. She loved the way it bathed her skin, and after a moment or two of acclimatising herself, she followed Jake's lead along the line of the reef.

It was spectacular. Straight away, she saw schools of fish swimming by. There were yellow-headed jaw fish, parrotfish and surgeon fish gliding amongst the coral.

The coral itself was exquisite. There were soft flowerlike fronds that waved with the motion of the water, and she recognised a type of sea fan with deep purple branches that looked as though it had been woven from lace. Feathery sea plumes were everywhere among the harder, stony species, but the staghorn coral was impressive with its antler-type formations.

She had been engrossed in her exploration, but Jake caught her attention, waving and pointing to somewhere behind her. She turned, slowly because of the ebb and flow of the water, and as she gazed around, she saw a loggerhead turtle swimming by.

She mimed her delight, and Jake responded by giving her a thumbs-up sign.

They swam on until they came across the anchor that Jake had told her about. It was covered with crustaceans, and Lacey was enthralled to see shrimp darting in and out of crevices between the heavy chain and the coral.

After about three quarters of an hour, Jake signalled to her that they should return to the surface. Their air tanks were running low, and it was essential that they get back to the boat in good time.

He reached the boat first and waited to give her a hand getting into it. On deck, they removed their diving equipment, and Lacey wrapped herself in a bath towel for a few minutes to dry off. Overhead, the sun was glorious in a startlingly blue sky, and she sat for a while on the bench seat, while Jake went into the galley to prepare drinks for both of them.

In the distance, where other boats were secured to various mooring buoys, people were enjoying the heat of the day, occasionally diving into the water to cool off. Some were snorkelling, whilst others were wearing scuba equipment.

'It's watermelon with a dash of Bacardi,' Jake said, coming back on deck and handing her a long, frosted glass. Ice cubes floated in the pink-coloured juice, and she sipped gratefully, savouring it as the cool liquid slid down her throat.

'I don't know whether you prefer to have lunch out here on deck, or in the cabin,' he said. 'It might be quite nice to sit here and dry off for a bit longer.'

'I'd like that,' she murmured. She tried not to notice his long, lithe body, bronzed by the sun, encased only in swim trunks that clung to his hips and emphasised his strongly muscled thighs. His shoulders were broad, and he had a six-pack that would have done justice to any male, god-like creature.

'Good. Then I'll be back in a minute or two.'

'Can I do anything to help?'

He shook his head. 'No, you stay there and dry yourself off. Everything's all prepared. It just needs to be put out.'

Lacey did as he suggested, and let the sun bathe her, loving the way it caressed her skin, warming her through and through. She placed her drinking glass in a custom-made drinks holder at the side of the bench, and then tilted her head back so that it rested on the cushioned headrest that had been thoughtfully built in. She stretched out her long legs. For the first time in months she felt truly relaxed, invigorated by the swim but comfortable in mind and body.

'Food's coming up,' Jake said. He was carrying a wicker hamper, which he placed down on the floor beside the bench, and then he went over to the opposite bench, lifted the seat and rummaged in the storage compartment.

'Foldaway table,' he said, coming back towards her in triumph. 'You shall have your meal in comfort.'

'I'm amazed,' she said, as he opened up the hamper a moment or two later and set out the dishes of food. 'You've thought of everything.'

There was a chilled fruit starter, a basket made from the scooped-out rind of a melon and filled with a medley of honeydew melon, star fruit, nectarines, grapes and blueberries.

Lacey stared at him. 'I can't believe you did all this yourself...did you?'

He smiled and made a play of covering his nose with his hand. 'Well, if I were Pinocchio, I'd be tempted to say yes, but then I might have to live with the consequences.' He looked at the beautifully presented basket. 'Actually, my housekeeper prepared everything. She loves cooking and as you can see, she's very good at it. Help yourself. Taste it. I think you'll agree she's found her place in life.'

Lacey savoured the food. There was rice and chicken, served with a delicious crisp salad, and there were *cubanos*, sandwiches made with crusty Cuban-style bread, filled with roast pork, ham, salami, cheese and pickle. The sandwiches had been pressed in a heated device that bound the ingredients together and allowed the flavours to come through. They ate them cold, but it didn't matter, because they were just as good as the hot version.

'And key lime pie to follow?' Lacey rolled her eyes. 'I think I must be in heaven.' The creamy yellow pie was topped with whipped cream, and the blend of sweet and tart tastes was incredible. 'You must thank your housekeeper for me and tell her that her food is delicious. At this rate, I shall be so stuffed you'll have to carry me home and roll me into bed,' she complained.

'Well, that's definitely an option,' Jake said with a laugh, and Lacey stared at him blankly until it dawned on her what she had said.

'No, I mean… I wasn't suggesting… I meant…'

'I know what you meant,' he said, his mouth curving. 'I just prefer my version, that's all.'

He was looking at her, the devil in his eyes, and the atmosphere crackled with electric tension. She felt heat sweep through her from the top of her head right down to her toes. How did he manage to do this to her? He only had to look at her and her nervous system kicked into action, making her heartbeat quicken and sending a rush of sensation to curl along her spine.

'I'm…uh…really glad that you brought me out here today,' she managed, searching for a way to defuse the situation. 'I loved being able to swim around the reef.'

'Well, it has to beat staying home and painting

the walls any day,' he said with a wry smile. 'I've caught glimpses of you wielding your paint roller in the mornings before you set off for work.'

She made a soft laugh. 'I didn't realise how many walls there were until I started.'

He nodded. 'They multiply in the night while you're sleeping.' His mouth tilted at the corners. 'I must say your house looked fresh and clean enough to me when I was there, but I suppose you're looking to change the colour scheme?'

'Just a little. I want cool magnolia instead of sunshine yellow. It's so hot some days that I need the extra help to keep the temperature down, mentally if not physically. And it's a way of making the house truly mine.'

'By putting your stamp on it, you mean?'

'That's right.'

'So you're not having second thoughts about selling up?' His gaze was thoughtful. 'I was kind of hoping you might have reconsidered by now. I'd be willing to offer you way above the market price.'

She frowned. 'I don't really understand why you're so keen on buying me out. I know you said it was to do with the land, but I imagine you could extend in the opposite direction if you wanted. I know it would take some work, clearing the land, and so on, but it is a possible option, surely?'

'I think the work would be too much to take on.' He leaned back in his seat. 'The truth is, my grandfather built the house you're living in now, some fifty or more years ago. It was the family home through three generations. When my father married my mother, my grandparents moved out and went to live in the house next door…where I live now.'

He frowned. 'My brother and I grew up in your house as kids. We loved it. All our memories were there, and there was a huge sense of satisfaction and appreciation because my grandfather had designed and built it especially for us. It was a bitter blow when the family decided they had to sell up.'

'Why would they do that, if it meant so much to them?'

'Because my grandfather's dream was to make the family's fortune by finding a wreck that he could salvage, and he needed funds to make one last attempt. He felt he was really close to finding what he was after. It was a passion that drove him on through a good many years, and it cost him a huge amount of time and money to fund the diving expeditions. He wouldn't give up. He knew his prize was out there somewhere, and he was determined to find it.'

'So your father sacrificed his home to fund your grandfather's dream? Wasn't that a lot to ask of him?'

Jake nodded. He lifted up his glass of chilled spritzer and took a long swallow, tilting his head back a fraction. Lacey watched in fascination as his throat moved, and then he laid the glass momentarily on his hot skin, taking relief from the coolness of the glass.

'It was,' he said, 'but in the end it was a family decision. They would all benefit if my grandfather's efforts were successful, and they backed him to the hilt. In the meantime, we all moved into the big house and waited to see what would happen.'

'And eventually your grandfather…' Lacey broke off as a commotion started up somewhere in the distance. She and Jake both glanced around to see what was going on, and it appeared that the shouting was coming from a boat moored across the bay.

'It looks as though someone's being pulled out of the water,' Jake said. 'A woman. She's wearing scuba equipment.'

'Is that blood I can see?' Lacey peered at the people on the boat, putting a hand to her forehead to shade out the sun.

'It looks like it.' He frowned. 'Perhaps we'd better go over there and see if we can help. The key to the medical cupboard is in the storage compartment alongside the wine chiller. We might need dressings and tape if they don't have any aboard their own boat.'

She nodded. Jake untied the boat and then took the helm, while Lacey went to check supplies. She was puzzled to see that he had a full stock of emergency medical equipment on board... the sort that qualified doctors might use.

She took the medical case out on deck. 'I don't understand,' she said. 'This equipment is so advanced. There are oxygen masks and suture kits...why would you have all this on board? I was expecting to find just first-aid dressings and antiseptic.'

He glanced at her briefly. 'I thought it might come in handy.'

Lacey frowned, but said no more as they moved alongside the other boat. By now, panic had set in amongst the people helping the injured woman. She had a neck wound, and was beginning to fade in and out of consciousness.

'It's gone right through an artery,' one man was saying, his voice threaded through with shock.

'How do we stop the flow? It's not happening. It's too deep.'

'Just keep the pressure on the wound while I get this scuba equipment off her.'

'Marie, can you hear me…? it's Ross… Stay with us. We're going to take care of you…' The voices drifting across the water were becoming more anxious with every second that passed.

Jake tied up the boat alongside them and called out. 'Hello, there. We're doctors. Is there anything we can do to help?'

Lacey stared at him. A doctor? Jake was a doctor? Had she heard him right?

'Thank heaven.' The man, Ross, was applying pressure to the woman's neck, but it didn't seem to be having much effect. 'Yes, anything you can do… It must have been the coral…she must have brushed up against it somehow… there's a gash right along her neck.'

'Okay, we'll come aboard. Call the emergency services.' He turned back to Lacey. 'Bring the medical bag. From the look of things, we'll need a Foley catheter and saline. Maybe a suture kit, too.'

'Perhaps I should deal with this,' she said. 'I'm the one who's working in emergency, after all.' He'd said he was a doctor, but how experienced was he, and what branch of medicine did he specialise in? How could he have given it all up to spend his days fishing and scubadiving?

'I'm still qualified,' he answered, his voice terse. 'I quit my job some time ago, but my licence is up to date.'

He wasn't giving way, it seemed, and Lacey realised that now wasn't the time to question him further. They had a patient to deal with. She said no more, but went on board with him and knelt down alongside the woman and began to check her condition.

Marie was in a desperate situation. If the blood loss continued at this rate she would soon lose consciousness altogether and her heart would fail. If they were to save her, something had to be done, fast.

Jake had already assessed the situation and was ready to act. 'I'm going to insert a catheter into the artery,' he explained to the anxious on-lookers, 'so that I can put a small balloon in place. Then I'll inflate the balloon with sterile saline and retract the catheter. With any luck it will stop the blood flow by compressing the blood vessel against the first rib.'

That made sound sense to Lacey. He certainly appeared to know what he was doing. 'I'll put in an intravenous line and start fluids,' she said. If they didn't quickly replace the blood Marie had lost, she would go into shock, and the consequences would be dire.

Jake nodded. He had the catheter in place by now, and was inflating the balloon, but the balloon was trying to escape the wound. His mouth tightened briefly. 'I'll have to suture it in place so that it doesn't dislodge on the way to hospital.'

Lacey watched as he made purse-string sutures to close up the skin. Throughout this drama he had worked with perfect expertise, not pausing for a moment. He knew exactly what to do, and he had not hesitated in the slightest. Lacey could only watch and wonder why on earth he had passed up on what was obviously his vocation.

'Is she going to be all right?' Ross was white faced, with lines of tension ingrained around his mouth.

'She's stabilised for now,' Jake answered. 'The bleeding has stopped, and we're replacing fluids she's lost, so that should keep her safe until we can get her to hospital. They'll take over and seal the blood vessel properly. I expect she'll go to Theatre for the procedure.'

'Thanks,' Ross said. 'Thanks to both of you for what you've done. I can't even think about what might have happened if you hadn't been close by.'

'I'm glad we could help.' Jake checked on his patient, whose eyes were beginning to flutter open. 'You'll be okay, Marie,' he told her. 'Just lie still and preserve your strength.'

He turned to look across the water as the hum of a motor launch sounded some distance away. It was coming towards them, and he told her quietly, 'This must be the rescue service. They'll take over now and see that you're taken safely to hospital.' Looking at Ross, he said, 'Perhaps you should gather a few belongings together if you want to go with her.'

'I'll do that.'

When the launch came to a stop alongside them, Jake explained the situation to the paramedics on board. 'The catheter is just a temporary measure,' he said. 'It was the only thing on hand that would solve the problem.'

'It looks as though it's working.' The paramedic smiled. 'We'll take care of her.' He turned to Marie. 'You've had a lucky escape there. Now let's get you to hospital. I'll bet this is one scuba trip that you'll remember for ever.'

They watched as the woman was laid on a stretcher and transported to the launch, and then Lacey tidied up the medical kit, preparing to leave. She and Jake said goodbye to the woman's friends. 'I'm sorry your trip had to end this way,' Jake murmured.

'At least she's alive. That's something to be thankful for.'

Lacey was subdued as they returned to Jake's boat. The accident had been a shocking, unexpected occurrence, and she was fairly certain that if Jake hadn't intervened the woman would not have survived this day. It made her wonder all the more why he had turned his back on medicine. His revelation had come out of the blue and she was reeling from the effects of it, even now.

'Perhaps we should head for home,' Jake said, glancing up at the sky. 'It looks as though we might be in for a brief squall, so it would be sensible to keep out of its way.'

She nodded. 'That's fine by me. After what just happened, anything else would seem like an anticlimax.' She studied him, wondering if he would offer any insight as to how he had come to end his medical career, but he remained steadfastly silent on the matter, and when she tried to broach the subject he simply batted it away.

'I don't practise medicine any more on a day-to-day basis,' he said, starting up the motor. 'It's as simple as that.'

She shook her head. 'There's nothing simple about it. You gave up on all those years of medical training… all that expertise is going to waste. How could you turn your back on your career that way?'

'I decided I'd had enough, and so I quit. That's all there is to it. I don't need to work for a living and I prefer things the way they are. I'm sorry if you don't like that, but that's how it is.'

His glance flicked over her. 'I prefer my lifestyle as it is now. This way I get to enjoy the beauty of the islands and spend time with a gorgeous girl.'

She pressed her lips together. 'I don't believe you could walk away from medicine just like that.'

'Believe it.' He sent her an oblique look. 'I've had a great time spending the day with you. And we still have a good half an hour or so left before we arrive back home…maybe that will be time enough for me to persuade you that you could benefit from selling to me.'

She frowned. 'You're avoiding the subject.'

'I'd rather talk about you. Just think what you could do with the money if you let the house go. You could buy a place nearer to your sister and her family and furnish it throughout. There would even be enough left over for a holiday, or whatever takes your fancy.'

Lacey didn't answer. Why was he doing this? Jake was a man of hidden depths and she simply didn't know what to make of him. He was fun to be with, and there was no denying she could easily fall for him big time. He was sexy with a bone-melting charisma, and above all he made it clear that he was attracted to her and seemed to genuinely want to be with her.

Even so, she was beset by doubts. Underlying all that was the knowledge that he kept coming back to this same issue...he wanted her house and land. He put the question to her whenever the opportunity arose.

Was this the real reason he had brought her out here today?

CHAPTER SIX

'So you went with Jake out to the reef?' Rob was clearly disgruntled. 'I'll bet he couldn't wait to show you the boat. He's been working on it for ages. Heaven knows why he wants another one, though. He'll soon be able to start his own fleet at this rate.'

Lacey chuckled. 'I can see you're in fine form today. It's just envy, you know. Maybe we'd all like a little of what he has.' She glanced at Rob's chart. His heart rate had settled to a normal rhythm, and his temperature and pulse were steadily reverting to a satisfactory reading. His blood pressure was still a little high, but with any luck the consultant would allow him to go home tomorrow.

'I don't know about that. I never envied anyone anything. Well, not to any great extent.' Rob grimaced. He was sitting in a chair by the bed, and she could see that he'd been reviewing some of his video footage from the trip to the Everglades. Even in hospital he couldn't stop working. No wonder he was having trouble with his blood pressure.

'It's all acquisition with him, isn't it?' he said. 'I expect he's been badgering you to sell the house to him, as well…he was always interested in it, I know. I used to see him eyeing up the boundary lines, as though he was mentally taking stock. He did say it was a prime site for oranges and limes, and even avocados, but he always seemed to me to be more interested in the house. Why would he want that when he lives in that grand place next door?'

'That's what I asked…but it seems there's a family connection to my house. His grandfather built it, and I think he feels emotionally attached to the place.'

Rob made a face. 'So do you, I imagine. It was your parents' holiday home, wasn't it? You must have lots of memories of you and Grace spending summers there.'

'I do, and that's what I told him. We spent such happy times together. My parents were so easy-going, allowing us enough freedom to spread our wings and try new things, but at the same time keeping an eye on us to make sure we were safe.'

Her expression was sad. 'I really miss them. I miss being able to ring them up and have a chat at any time, or drop by their house for Sunday lunch. Now that's all changed, and this is the only place I have to remember them by. With Grace living here in the States, it seemed the best option to keep this property rather than the one in the UK.'

She stopped to forage in her bag. 'I brought some reading for you.' She placed some fresh newspapers on the table at the end of his bed. 'It's a difficult situation, and in a way I feel guilty about holding out against Jake, but I don't want to give up the house. After all, it's not as though he's far removed from his birthplace, is it? He sees it every day.'

'You should stick to your guns. You have as much reason to be there as he does.'

She nodded. 'I tried to make him see that, but I'm not sure he was convinced.' She straightened, and braced herself, getting ready to leave. 'Anyway, I must get back to work. Just remember to give me a call when the consultant says you can go home, and I'll come and fetch you. I've made your old room ready for you so you can stay there until they sort out what's going on with your heart and what needs to be done about it.'

'Thanks, Lacey. You're an angel.'

'Yeah, sure I am.' She grinned and left the room, getting ready to finish her stint in the emergency department.

It was business as usual. 'Non-stop trauma all day,' Emma greeted her, with a frown. 'You'd think people would take more care, wouldn't you…? But, no, we have traffic accidents, industrial accidents and disasters at sea, day in and day out.' She handed Lacey a chart, along with an X-ray film. 'Broken ribs in treatment room two. His breathing's poor and he's very uncomfortable. Shall I call a surgeon to consult?'

Lacey flipped the film into the light box. She nodded. 'Yes, call the surgeon. It looks like a flail chest, where a segment of the rib cage has come adrift, and it seems there's some damage to the lung underneath. In the meantime, I'll need to put in a chest tube to clear the blood that's accumulating and help him to breathe more easily. Will you be free to help me with that?'

'Yes, I will. I'll go and set up the equipment.' Emma glanced at Lacey before leaving. 'I hear you rescued a woman the other day out on the reef. She's recovered well by all accounts.'

'So I heard, though actually it was my neighbour, Jake, who did the rescuing. He was brilliant from start to finish, taking the situation in hand and saving the day. He didn't even stop to think, but everything he did was smooth and efficient and made a real difference to the final outcome.'

'Jake Randall, is that right? I know him. He used to work here. He was a great doctor, one of the best, but he quit at the end of the year and didn't come back, and I was so sad when he left. He got on well with everyone.' She made a faint smile. 'There were some broken hearts among the female staff around here, I can tell you.'

'I can imagine. He seems to have that effect on people.' Lacey didn't want to think about how many women had fallen for Jake. It was his easygoing manner, his inherent charm and dry sense of humour, perhaps, that caused the domino effect, and she was certainly not immune. Still, it was interesting to learn that he had worked here.

She removed the X-ray from the light box and went with Emma to tend to her patient. Keeping busy was the best thing to do. That way her head wasn't being constantly overloaded with thoughts of Jake and his exploits. Fortunately, too, it meant that the rest of the day rushed by until finally her shift came to an end.

'I won't be in tomorrow,' she told Emma. 'I have a four-day break and when I come back I'll be on the early shift. In the meantime, Dr Mayfield will be in charge. If there are any problems with any of my patients, refer them to him, or to Mike, the attending physician… but you have my number in case of any queries, don't you?'

Emma nodded. 'We'll be fine.' She smiled. 'It's great having you around, Lacey. You've slotted in here as though you've been here all your life.'

'It feels that way sometimes.' Lacey grinned. 'See you.'

She drove home along the main highway, contemplating the day's events. It was deeply satisfying working in Emergency, and as each day ended she was tired and ready to fall into a deep sleep. She was looking forward to these few days off, though. Grace was coming over with the children, and it would be great to get together again as a family.

Once she was home, she went into the kitchen and made herself a cup of coffee and a toasted sandwich. She took them out onto the deck and sat looking out over the garden, which was dimly lit in the moonlight. Beyond the garden were several acres of land that belonged to her, land that was still in its natural state, bounded by woods and mangrove swamps. It was eerie in the darkness, even though the lamp on the deck sent out a golden pool of light.

She could just make out shadows of the shrubbery, and in the distance the trees of the orange grove. Their scent wafted faintly on the air. Earlier in the day she had plucked grapefruit, mangoes and oranges, and her fridge was filled with fruit that would refresh her throughout the following week. Being here was like living in paradise, with nature providing everything she might need.

Now, though, her thoughts were distracted by an odd sound coming from somewhere in the far reaches of the property. She couldn't quite make it out. There were muffled thuds and an odd scraping sound like a shovel breaking into earth or faintly clanging against tree bark. Then the tree branches in the distance seemed to move, and in a break in the undergrowth a black shadow flitted against the skyline.

'Jake, is that you?' She called out into the darkness. Why would Jake be roaming the boundaries of her land? 'Jake?'

There was more rustling. She thought she heard a muffled curse, and then there was the crackle of vegetation underfoot. 'Jake? Are you out there? What's going on? What are you doing?'

Silence. Nothing stirred and then a bird startled her, flapping its huge wings as it took off from a mangrove tree, making a stark silhouette against the night sky.

Lacey's heart was beginning to pound. Why

wasn't Jake answering? Who was out there? If it wasn't Jake, why were they on her land? Ought she to go and take a look?

For the first time she was truly conscious of how far she was from the nearest property. Jake's was the only house for at least a mile, and he wasn't answering her. How would she protect herself if anyone meant to do her harm?

She picked up her phone from the table and hesitated. It was one thing to face up to an intruder in an area that was well lit, but darkness gave the venture a very different perspective and she didn't want to blunder about in the shadowy undergrowth, not knowing where she was going or what she might run into.

A shiver ran the length of her spine, and she realised that her hands were shaking. What was the matter with her? Surely, she was imagining things? It must have been a simple night noise, an animal, a deer, perhaps, that had been wandering about in the woods and had blundered onto her land.

Anyway, if there really was an intruder, she could ring Jake at home, couldn't she? Hearing his voice would at least put her mind at ease. He would probably think she was being foolish, but that didn't matter too much, did it?

He wouldn't hesitate to come and help out, she was certain, and with him by her side she could face up to anything. Between them they could find out what was going on.

She dialled his number and waited. The phone rang for some time, but there was no answer, and tension began to build up inside her. She frowned. Was he out? Suddenly, she felt truly alone.

In the end, she cut the call and went inside the house, locking all the doors and making certain that everything was secure. She would check the fences in the morning. Her nerves were a mess. Perhaps it came from drinking too much coffee, and the fact that she had been at work all day, and her thoughts were taken up with this business of the house. She was overtired and her mind was playing tricks on her. What she needed was a good night's sleep.

It was just as well she had come inside the house, she decided. She wasn't up to dealing with problems right now. She felt apprehensive, insecure and totally unlike her usual self. Even in bed she was haunted by night terrors.

Her slumber was fitful, her dreams filled with shadowy figures and feral screeches, and in the morning, when she clambered out of bed, she felt decidedly rough.

A shower didn't help very much, neither did her first cup of coffee of the day, but she had promised that she would go and fetch Rob from the hospital at the earliest opportunity so she steeled herself to get organised. She made do with a cereal bar for breakfast, not wanting to keep him waiting. Knowing Rob, he would be packed and ready and chafing at the bit to get out of there.

He was in much better spirits than she might have expected when she arrived at the hospital.

'It's just so great to be getting out of this place,' he said. 'No offence, but hospitals freak me out. I don't like being cooped up, and I can't stand the smell of antiseptic.'

'A lot of people feel the same way,' Lacey conceded. 'Still, if it saves your life or puts your health back on track, who's to complain?'

'Me?' He grinned, raising a brow in query. 'I know I've been grumbling a lot lately. It's just that I have strong opinions and I like to be on the move, so being stuck in hospital brought out all my frustration and turned me into a grouch. I shouldn't do it. I know it isn't fair…especially when you've been so great, coming to visit, and now you're having to act as a taxi service.' He glanced at her, his eyes narrowing a fraction. 'Actually, you're looking a bit peaky. Are you okay?'

'I'm fine,' she said. 'I've a bit of a headache, that's all. Anyway, let's head for home and you can edit your films to your heart's content. Everything's ready for you in the guest bedroom.'

'That's great. You don't know how much it means to me to be able to come back to your place for a while. The consultant wanted me to stay local until this problem with the heart is diagnosed properly... And, of course, that means monitoring what's happening. It's like finding an intermittent fault in an electrical system... until the unit fails, you don't know where the problem lies. At least, that's how he explained it to me.'

'Not that we're expecting your heart to fail.' She laughed. 'It's just that the wiring seems to be a little faulty right now.'

'True.' He settled back in the seat of her car and watched the scenery go by. The journey didn't take long, and soon they were back at the house.

She poured cold drinks from the fridge, and they talked for a while in the living room, until Rob asked, 'Do you mind if I go along to my room and sort through my work stuff? I'll come and join you in a while, but there are one or two jobs I need to get on with. I haven't had access to a decent computer for a while and it's been driving me crazy.'

'You go ahead,' she told him. 'I can see you're itching to get back to work, and I have lots of things to do. I'll give you a shout when lunch is ready.'

'Thanks, Lacey.' He hurried away to the bedroom, leaving Lacey to catch up with chores around the house. She wanted to prepare the other two bedrooms for Grace and the children. They should be arriving later on today, and she was keen to have everything ready for them.

A couple of hours later, she was back in the kitchen, trying to decide what she should prepare for lunch. Tiredness was rapidly getting the better of her, and she realised it was probably lack of food that was contributing to her lacklustre manner.

Rob, sitting at the kitchen table, leafing through a camera magazine, was no help at all.

'Anything would be good after hospital food,' he said. 'When I lived here on my own, I survived on pizza and takeaways and whatever convenience foods I could find stashed in the freezer.'

'You're a culinary wasteland,' she said with a wry smile. 'It's a good thing I have a couple of weeks to re-educate you on the right way of doing things.'

The doorbell rang as she gazed into the fridge for inspiration. Lacey frowned. 'I don't know who that can be,' she murmured. 'Unless, of course, it's Jake.' Her brow knotted. Why would Jake be here?

She went out of the room and hurried along the corridor to the front door. Sure enough, Jake was waiting in her porch, and she gazed at him for a moment or two, wondering what he was doing there. He, in turn, gave her an assessing look and frowned.

'What's wrong, Lacey? You're very pale.' He looked at her more closely. 'There are shadows under your eyes. Are you coming down with something?'

She shook her head. 'No, I'm fine. It's lack of sleep, that's all. Perhaps I was sitting out on the deck too late last night.'

'If you say so.' He gave her a doubtful look. 'Is anything in particular stopping you from sleeping? Is there anything I can get you to perk you up a bit?'

'No, to both of those questions, thanks all the same.' There was no point in telling him about her fears from the night before. He would put it down to her imagination, or a stray animal, much as she had done. She frowned. 'Why are you here, Jake? Was there something you wanted?'

'Ah, yes. I brought you a small offering.' He lifted up a cool-bag, adding, 'My housekeeper, Jane, made you a seafood platter and a fruit tart for afters. She was really pleased that you were kind enough to compliment her on her food after the boat trip the other day, and she wanted me to give these to you. She made them specially.'

Lacey looked inside the bag at the huge platter of food and the colourful fruit tart with its perfect glazed finish. 'Oh, how lovely.' She lifted her gaze to Jake. 'It was so thoughtful of her to do that.'

'Well, the added factor is that she heard that Rob might be coming home today, and she knows he's partial to seafood. I think she has a soft spot for him and wants to make sure he's looking after himself properly, so from time to time she bakes him a pie, or whatever.'

'She's right—Rob's home from hospital. He's in the kitchen right now.' She stood aside to let him into the house. 'Please thank Jane for me again. This has cheered me up so much.'

'Did you need cheering up? What's wrong?'

'Like I said, nothing. Nothing that I want to talk about, anyway.'

'Hmm.' He studied her, as though he was trying to fathom her mood. 'You know I'm always here for you if you need me…if anything troubles you, or spooks you in any way you only have to call on me.' He paused, thinking things through. 'You said you were out on the deck last night—we're a bit isolated out here, and the sounds coming from all around late at night can seem very different from what you hear in the daytime. It can all feel a bit scary, especially if you'rc overtired.'

'Yes, that's true.' Lacey's brows drew together. Why had he mentioned that particular worry? Had he been the one in the woods last night? And if so, why hadn't he answered her shouts?

They walked through to the kitchen and Jake set the bag down on the table, nodding a greeting towards Rob. 'I brought a food parcel from Jane,' he said with a grin. 'She's convinced you might fade away without a good helping of her food inside you. I told her she was wasting gourmet food on a pizza and burgers fanatic, but there we are. Who am I to argue with a woman when she's set her heart on something?'

Rob tried out a smile. 'I do appreciate Jane's cooking. I'm sure she understands that.'

'Maybe.'

Lacey waved Jake towards a seat. 'We were just wondering what to have for lunch, and now you've solved our problem. Will you join us? It looks as though there's enough food here to feed a platoon.'

She frowned. Rob might not be too happy at the situation…but maybe it was time the two of them declared a truce. If they never sat down together and talked, how were they going to resolve their problems with one another?

'Thanks, I'd like that very much, if you're sure it's all right?' Jake was asking Lacey, but his glance diverted towards Rob.

Rob gave a negligent shrug. 'It's fine by me.'

'Good.'

'That's settled, then. I'll make a salad to go with it.' Lacey set about preparing a colourful

addition to the meal, using crisp lettuce, crou-
tons, eggs and Parmesan cheese, all combined
with a creamy mustard dressing.

'Were you home last night?' she asked, looking at Jake. 'I saw that your lights were on, but
that didn't necessarily mean that you were at
home.'

He nodded. 'I was in my study, looking
through the old plans showing the layout of your
house. I could let you have them, if you like.
My grandfather kept them out of nostalgia, I
suppose, since he always hoped that he would
one day buy the property back. In fact, he and
my parents tried to do that several times, but
they were unsuccessful. Still, they never gave
up. There was some hope that my brother might
bring his family to live here at some point, and
that way the whole estate would eventually be
combined as one.'

'Oh, I see.' She frowned and began to set the
food out on the table.

'Well, no matter,' Jake said, 'but the plans

are interesting. They show the areas that were once covered in water and the land that has been reclaimed through planting schemes. He even noted the crags and rock formations that form one section of the boundary. There are small caves and inlets where the water once encroached...but I don't suppose you've had time to explore every section yet, have you?'

'No, I haven't.' Lacey pulled a bottle of light white wine from the fridge and handed it to Rob so that he could uncork it. 'I went over every inch of the place when I was younger, of course, but I think a lot of it is overgrown now, with creepers and new tree growth. I thought about clearing some of it away some time, but actually I'm quite pleased with the natural look of the place.'

She darted him a quick look. 'I rang you last night, but you didn't answer.' Feigning unconcern, she watched his expression surreptitiously while she added the finishing touches to the table.

'Really? I'm sorry about that.' He frowned. 'I sometimes switch my phone off when I don't want to be disturbed...and for some reason my voice mail wasn't working... I had no idea you were trying to get in touch. Was something wrong?'

She shook her head, wondering how she would explain her call, especially since she didn't want to give Rob any cause for concern. 'I just wanted to let you know that our scubadiving patient was on the mend. They discharged her from hospital the day before yesterday.'

'That's great news.' He smiled. 'I'm glad. And as to the phone, I'll be sure to leave it switched on now, in case you call...although you can always reach me by my landline. I'll give you the number.'

She didn't know whether to be reassured or not. The whole incident had disturbed her, much as she tried to tell herself it was probably a figment of her imagination.

'We should eat,' she said, sitting down at the table. 'Help yourselves.'

They all tucked in. The fish platter was truly wonderful, with oysters, clams, shrimp and conch fritters, served alongside rice and vegetables. Jane had created the perfect meal.

'So how are you feeling?' Jake asked, giving Rob a thoughtful glance. 'You've been through the mill a bit lately, haven't you?'

'I'm fine.' Rob was clearly uncomfortable discussing his health with another man. 'I just want to get back to work.'

'That's good.' Jake speared shrimp with his fork. 'I don't know whether you'd be interested in this, but my brother put forward an idea for a TV or film documentary about exploration of the wrecks in the area. Some of our salvage operations would make good viewing, and a lot of people are interested in recovered treasure and the way the recovery is carried out. We thought about commissioning a series of programmes that we could market to various media companies. Is that the sort of thing that you would be interested in?'

Rob was clearly taken with the idea. He was suddenly alert, wanting to know the ins and outs of the proposal. 'Are you suggesting that I should do the filming?'

Jake nodded. 'It's what you do best, isn't it? I've seen some of your documentaries, and you're beginning to make a name for yourself in the industry. You seem to have an eye for what will capture people's attention and keep them wanting more. What do you think—would you be prepared to do the filming?'

'I'd certainly be interested.' Rob's eyes were shining with enthusiasm. 'Perhaps we should get together some time and sift through a few ideas?'

Jake nodded. 'Tomorrow, perhaps at my place? My brother will be coming over in the morning, so we could decide together what we want.'

'That'll be great.' Rob was thoughtful as he

ate his salad. He was clearly working out a plan of action.

Jake turned his attention to Lacey. 'So when does your sister arrive?'

'Some time tonight. It'll be fairly late, so I expect the children will be tired…still, I've made everything ready for them. I've dug out a couple of trendy duvets—pretty princess for Cassie, and space rockets for Tom, so they should make a good first impression. And I managed to pick up a few toys and books from a stall in town, so that should help things along, too.'

'It sounds as though you're looking forward to seeing them. How old are they?'

'Cassie's six, and Tom is four. Cassie's very much the big sister, and Tom is every bit a boy… out to make his mark on the world. He's very inquisitive and wants to explore everything. It's been a few months since we last met up, and I've really missed seeing them.'

Jake's brows drew together. 'Obviously, you like having family around you. I do, too, but

I'm not so sure about children… My only experience has been with kids at the hospital… those in the waiting room can be a nightmare sometimes, running riot when their parents are distracted. And they always ask such awkward questions like, "Is he going to die?" "Why did you just drop that metal thing?" "Have you had your dinner in the hospital café? 'Cos my mum did, and she just threw up."'

Lacey chuckled. 'Children are very observant, I grant you that, and their minds are always ticking over, trying to work things out.' She studied him thoughtfully. 'I guess you're not planning on having a family of your own any time soon. It doesn't sound as though you're the settling-down type.'

His mouth twisted. 'Well, I have to say, children aren't very high on my list of priorities.' He returned her gaze. 'What about you? Has your experience with your ex put you off relationships for the foreseeable future?'

She thought about that. 'The truth is, I'm not

altogether sure. The last two years have been difficult for me, one way and another, and I'm just not clear about what I want these days. I've always wanted to have children… I don't think I can contemplate life without them, but the way things are that isn't likely to happen any time soon.'

Rob poured wine into her glass. 'You won't always feel this way. Life is something that happens to us, and we just make the best of it. Sooner or later things will drop into place and you'll look at them with a different eye. You just need to find the right man.' He glanced at Jake and there was a look that passed between them, a very male glance that spoke of rivalry and contention, as though a challenge had been thrown out.

'Maybe. In the meantime, I'll make do with a second-hand family, and enjoy the get-together when my sister and her offspring arrive.'

She turned her attention to the food. It was better not to think about Jake's aversion to settling down. She was drawn to him, there was no doubt about that, but nothing would ever come of it. They were miles apart in their outlook on life.

She cut a slice of the fruit pie and added cream. It was a joy to eat, with fresh, succulent pears and peaches, topped with lush strawberries, and the pastry melted in the mouth. 'You must thank Jane for me once again,' she told Jake. 'I can't help but think you're luckier than most, having her all to yourself. Maybe one day I'll meet with her and thank her in person.'

He smiled. 'I'm sure we can arrange that.'

They finished the meal, chatting lightly about this and that, and Lacey began to clear away the dishes, stacking them in the dishwasher. Jake offered to lend a hand, whilst Rob was busy drawing up plans for his next project.

Jake's phone rang as they were preparing to go outside onto the deck. While he answered the call, Lacey looked out over the grounds, her gaze going to the farthest extent her land, much of it hidden from view by the orange grove and distant rocky outcrops. Beyond those were the mangroves that grew along the channel that bordered her property.

She had checked the fences a few hours ago, and found several parts where an intruder could have slipped through. Some of the natural vegetation had been broken down and trampled, and that worried her because it meant that someone or something had been there. A frisson of cold ran through her body. It was disturbing how the fears of the night kept coming back to haunt her.

A note of tension in Jake's voice alerted her all at once, and she turned towards him.

'What's his condition?' Jake was saying. 'Is he having any trouble with his breathing? Any dizziness?' He frowned. 'Okay, then, tell them to lay him down on his back and give him oxygen. If it looks as though he's going to be sick they need to turn him over onto his side and make sure his airway is clear. If he stops breathing they should start CPR. I'll be with them in about ten minutes.'

Jake cut the call and said, 'I have to go. The emergency service has been in touch to say that a diver is in difficulties out in the bay. I'm probably nearest, so I'll be able to get to him first.'

'Is it bad?' Rob asked. 'What's happened?'

'I think he's probably suffering from the bends. He may have been in the water too long, or perhaps he surfaced too quickly. Either way, he's in trouble.'

He was already on the move, heading for the door, and Lacey followed him. 'Do you work for the rescue services?' she asked. She was puzzled. 'I thought you had given up medicine.'

'I only go out if it's local, or if there's a major disaster like a hurricane…which is a rare occurrence, thankfully. It helps that I have the boats. It gives me better access when there's a problem out at sea.'

'Could I come with you? I'd like to help.'

'Yes, of course.'

'Good luck,' Rob said. 'I hope things go well.'

They left him to go on with his work plans, while they hurried out to the dock.

Jake had the boat running within a minute. He was very quiet, and Lacey wondered if he was concerned for the diver, or whether he had other things on his mind.

As they sped out across the bay, though, she asked him, 'What happens when someone has the bends? I've never come across it before.'

He checked the co-ordinates he had been given and turned the boat in the direction of a nearby reef. 'It's to do with the way the body tissues absorb nitrogen from the breathing gas in proportion to the surrounding pressure. If the pressure is reduced too quickly, the nitrogen comes out of solution and forms bubbles in the body tissues. This causes the classic pain in the joints, but if the air bubbles enter the circulation as well, they might enter the lungs and

cause congestive symptoms and even circula-
tory shock through an arterial gas embolism.'

'So that's why we need to get to him fast, to
try to prevent that from happening?'

'Yes. If decompression sickness isn't treated
quickly, the diver could end up suffering from
brain damage, or he may not even survive.'

'But you told them to give him oxygen. Won't
that help? Won't that stop any of those symptoms developing?'

'Not necessarily. It will help, but people can
seemingly recover and then collapse later. He
needs decompression treatment if he's to be safe,
but the nearest hyperbaric chamber is at Key
Largo.'

'Will you be taking him there?'

'No. The rescue services will scramble a
launch to take him there, but it will take a while
to reach him. That's why we need to make sure
that his condition is stabilised before he starts
the journey.'

When they reached the mooring buoy some

five minutes later, it was clear that their patient was in a bad way. Jake and Lacey clambered aboard the diver's boat.

'He's not been making much sense at all,' a man told them. 'I know he's in pain,' he added in a low voice, 'and that's worrying, because Martin's not one to complain. He's finding it hard to get his breath as well. That means it's bad, doesn't it?'

'At least he's still conscious,' Jake murmured, kneeling down beside the patient, who was lying on the deck.

'Martin,' he said, 'I'm Jake Randall… I'm a doctor… Can you hear me?'

Martin mumbled a reply, but it was indistinct, and Jake tried again. 'You've been in a diving accident,' he said. 'You're suffering from decompression sickness… Do you understand what I'm saying?'

Martin's whole body was suddenly racked with tremors. He tried to answer, but clearly he was confused, and then he started to cough, an unhealthy sound, as though his lungs were filling up with fluid.

Jake turned to Lacey, who had come to kneel beside him. 'Will you go on giving him oxygen while I set up an intravenous line?' he asked. 'I'm going to give him isotonic fluids without dextrose to correct any dehydration and maintain blood pressure. I think we're going to have to put a urinary catheter in place as well.'

He glanced around at the people who were waiting anxiously on deck. 'Do you want to go into the cabin and give Martin some privacy while we do that? It would be helpful if you would call the Divers Alert Network—their number's on my phone.' He handed his mobile to the man who had been helping Martin. 'Tell them he definitely needs treatment in a hyperbaric chamber. They'll start making the necessary arrangements.'

'Okay, leave it with me.'

'Good…and keep the line open so they can get back in touch.'

'Will do.'

Lacey and Jake continued to work on their patient until they were satisfied they had done all they could for him, but just as they were beginning to feel it might be safe to sit back and wait for the rescue launch, Martin slipped into unconsciousness.

Jake examined him once more and then looked up at Lacey, his face grim. 'He's not breathing, and I can't find a pulse,' he said, his voice taut. 'We need to start CPR. Will you do chest compressions while I intubate him?'

Lacey nodded, and positioned herself so that she could press down on Martin's chest. Jake put a tube down his throat to help with his breathing, and as soon as that was in place he brought out the defibrillator.

Jake quickly fixed the pads in place on Martin's chest and switched on the machine. The man's heart had slipped into a dangerous rhythm.

'Charging,' Jake said, and then, 'Stand clear.' The defibrillator delivered an electric shock that was meant to restore Martin's heart rhythm to normal, but it failed. The heart monitor showed that he was still in a hazardous condition.

'I'll try again,' Jake said. His expression was bleak. His face was pale, his features grimly etched, and Lacey realised that she had never seen him this way before.

A second shock, but there was still nothing… no change.

Jake was doing everything he could for this man, but if this dangerous rhythm continued any longer, Martin could go into cardiac arrest. If he flat-lined, that would be the end. Jake knew it and Lacey knew it. She wished there was something she could do that would change the course of events, but she was helpless.

'Stand clear.' Another shock, and this time the heart trace began to show a sinus rhythm and Lacey breathed a sigh of relief. Martin was out of danger for the moment, at least.

Jake, though, was rigid with tension. He appeared to be completely drained of energy, his face shadowed, his clamped lips making it seem as though he was under great stress. It was clear that he was badly disturbed by everything that had gone on.

Lacey looked at him in concern. 'Jake, are you all right?'

'I'm okay,' he said.

She frowned. He wasn't okay at all. That was plain to see. Something was definitely wrong, and he was in denial. She desperately wanted to find out what was causing his tension so that she could find a way of helping him.

CHAPTER SEVEN

'YOU saved Martin's life, and yet you look as though you've gone into shock.' Lacey watched Jake as he eased himself away from the patient and checked the man's vital signs. 'I know something's wrong. Can you tell me about it? What's troubling you, Jake?'

'Nothing. And we can't waste time talking about it now.' He kept his voice low. 'We have to get Martin off this boat and on his way to Key Largo.' He looked at his watch. Every movement he made was stiff, as though it took a great effort. 'The launch should have been here by now…every second counts. The sooner he goes into decompression, the better his chances.'

'It's only been a few minutes,' Lacey said in a soothing tone. 'He's stable for the moment, and he'll be at the hospital within the hour.

That's all anyone can ask. Don't beat yourself up about it.'

'I'm not.' He made a ragged sigh. 'I just can't get used to the way life can be snatched away from people in a sudden accident or by a freak of nature. It's unfair. There's no coming to terms with it.' He gazed at her. 'But you already know that. You've been through it.'

'Yes, but you do come to terms with it in the end. You look back on the way people lived their lives and you celebrate the good times that live on in your memory.'

She watched his expression, but his features were still frozen into a taut mask. 'Are you feeling this way because of what happened to your parents? You said they had passed on…is that what troubles you?'

He shook his head. 'No. Obviously, yes, in part, it's unbearably sad, but they each had illnesses that gave them time to say their goodbyes. They loved one another to the end and shared a good life together. There were no regrets, no things left undone or words not said… In a way, they made it easier for my brother and me.'

'Then what—?' Lacey broke off as the engine of a motor launch sounded in the distance. It was coming nearer at speed.

Jake straightened up and checked his patient once more. 'His vital signs are holding steady,' he said.

'That's something, at least.' Lacey stood up. Much as she wanted to talk to Jake, she realised that he was right, and this was not the time to pursue things any further. Their priority had to be the patient, and so she went to talk to the anxious group of divers who were waiting to hear what was happening.

'He'll be given hyperbaric oxygen therapy,' she told them. 'That means oxygen will get to any damaged tissue and help with the healing process. Any bubbles of gas will be eliminated from his system, and he should slowly begin to recover.'

'How long will he be in there?'

'I don't know the answer to that, I'm afraid. You'll have to ask the doctor doing the hyperbaric treatment for his opinion…but usually treatment takes between several hours and a few days.' She sent the man a reassuring glance. 'He'll be all right in the hyperbaric chamber. Patients can talk to their therapist while they're in there, and in some instances they can even watch TV. So you needn't be concerned from that point of view.'

'No. You're probably right. Thanks.'

Lacey went to help supervise Martin's transfer to the launch. There was a doctor on board who was familiar with diving illnesses, and she felt confident that they were leaving him in good hands.

'I'll let you know how he gets on,' the doctor said as the launch started to move away.

Jake nodded. 'Thanks.'

Their job was done, and after a few minutes more they said goodbye to the people left behind on the boat. 'Make sure your equipment is up to date,' Jake advised them. 'You can buy gadgets that warn you if you're spending too long under water, or if you're coming up to the surface too fast. It's well worth spending the money on them if it saves a life.'

'We'll look into it.' The divers were subdued. Their friend had been in mortal danger and now a pall hung over the whole expedition.

'We should start back,' Jake said. His face was devoid of expression, as though he was getting by on automatic reflexes. 'Rob will be wondering what's happening, and I imagine your sister will be on her way to see you.'

'Yes.' Lacey went aboard the boat with him once more, and they watched as the divers set off for Key Largo. 'Perhaps we should take a few minutes to relax first, though,' she murmured. 'Come into the cabin and I'll make some tea. Having a hot drink might make you feel better.'

He didn't argue with her, and she guessed that was a measure of how low he was feeling. He seemed uptight, pacing up and down the small cabin like a caged animal, until she said quietly, 'Jake, you need to sit down… Take a seat and try to drink your tea while it's hot.'

He gazed at her blankly, then as she placed a hand on his shoulder and gently pressured him towards the bench, he gave in and did as she suggested. He rubbed a hand over his forehead.

'I'm sorry if I worried you,' he said. 'I wasn't really prepared for what happened today and it threw me for a while. I've been out to accidents before, but not to a case of decompression sickness…not in the last year, anyway.'

She was puzzled. 'I thought you handled everything perfectly.' She studied him carefully, taking in his braced, upright stance. He looked as though he was struggling to hold everything together.

She slid into the seat beside him. 'What more could you have done? As it is, he'll probably be back to full fitness within a couple of weeks, and that's all thanks to your swift actions.'

She frowned. 'You're a good doctor, Jake. I've seen it for myself, and I've heard other people say the same. I just don't understand how you could doubt yourself or turn your back on the profession you trained for.' She ran a hand over his arm, gently persuading him to look at her. 'What happened, Jake? Can you tell me? Is there something about this particular accident that bothers you?'

He sighed heavily and then nodded. 'My cousin had the same illness—decompression sickness. He was diving at one of our wreck sites, about eighteen months ago, and he must have stayed down there too long. When his fellow divers realised he was in difficulty, they hurried to bring him out of the water as soon as possible, but he was already unconscious. They tried everything they could to resuscitate him, but it was no use. He died.'

She made a soft gasp. 'Oh, Jake, I'm so sorry. That must have been awful for you.' She reached for him, putting her arms around him as his shoulders slumped. 'Were you there when it happened?'

He shook his head. 'I was at work, at the hospital, but as soon as I heard he was in trouble I took the boat out to the wreck site. They were still working on him when I arrived there, but I could see it was too late. His heart had stopped and the doctors tried everything they could to revive him, but it was impossible. There was nothing anyone could do.'

She wrapped her arms more firmly around him, drawing him close, so that his cheek was next to hers and the warmth of her body would comfort him. She felt the heavy thud of his heartbeat next to hers, and for just a few minutes they stayed like that, locked together in each other's arms.

'You must have been very close to him,' she said softly. 'Did you ever go on dives with him?'

He nodded. 'We were practically inseparable as youngsters, and that carried on into adulthood. He loved diving, and he always felt that he was contributing to the family's fortunes by unearthing artefacts from the wrecks.' He made a brief smile. 'Once he found a beautiful gold cross, encrusted with emeralds… There was some talk of selling it, but we didn't…we'd already made millions, and it wasn't necessary… So now it's part of our collection, and I'm just thankful that we have it as a physical memento of the work he put in at the wrecks.'

'Did you dive on a regular basis?'

'Only when I wasn't working at the hospital. I made a number of finds, and they were added to the collection, but I value them more for their history than anything else. This whole area is steeped in history…the era of sailing ships, their crews, and pirates. My grandfather was excited by all that, and his enthusiasm was infectious. It was passed down through our family.' His mouth flattened. 'I shared his feelings to begin with, and I have a lot to be grateful for, but now I simply want to preserve his legacy. I want to make sure that the company he set up thrives, so that my cousin's death won't have been in vain.'

He frowned. 'I was never wholly involved in the venture. I moved away from the family business and went into medicine.'

'And yet you gave that up.'

'Yes.' He straightened and Lacey let her arms fall to her sides. She felt bereft for a moment, feeling the loss of his warmth, of his strong male body next to hers.

He took her hand in his. 'I know you'll find this hard to understand…but after my cousin died everything seemed pointless. You work hard, you do your best for your family, for other people, and yet life can be plucked away from you in a second. Why put in all that effort if it's not going to do any good? We might as well enjoy life while we can, because you never know what's around the corner.'

'I do understand.' She looked up at him, her gaze troubled as she studied his bleak expres-

sion. 'It's just that I think life is all about helping one another, and if you have a skill that can
make someone else's life better, then it doesn't
seem right not to use it.'

He leaned towards her and kissed her gently
on the mouth. 'You're very sweet. I'm glad that
you came to live next door.' His glance moved
over her, lingering on the soft fullness of her
lips, and it was just as though he had kissed
her again. Lacey felt the lasting impression of
that kiss as though he had seared her with his
touch.

'I'll take you home,' he said. 'It'll be good for
you to have your family with you…and it'll keep
Rob from making any untoward moves in your
direction.' His eyes glinted in the soft light of
the cabin.

She stared at him, her mouth dropping open
a little. 'You men,' she said in protest. 'You're
unbelievable. All this sniping at one another,
when I've made it quite clear I've no intention

of dating any man right now. You should take a break, the pair of you.'

He laughed softly. 'I'm fine with that. Because I'm sure that eventually I'll be able to persuade you to change your mind.'

She shook her head and stood up, sliding out from the bench and going to take the air outside on deck. It was impossible to deal with him. Just a few minutes ago he had shown her another side to him, the part of him that could be hurt, the part that grieved for what he could not bring back, and yet now he was teasing her, making a play for her as if nothing had happened.

She didn't know what to make of him. Was it bravado, a reckless attempt to gloss over the worries that lay beneath the surface? Was his laid-back style, his live-for-the-moment attitude, just a front?

They set off, heading back over the water for the secluded dock that was shared by both properties. Jake secured the boat and then saw her to her door, saying lightly, 'Thanks for helping me out with Martin. You'd make a good first-on-the-scene doctor if you ever consider a career change.'

She smiled. 'Thanks, but I'm happy as I am.'

He left her, and she let herself into the house, going to find Rob to tell him about the incident. 'I think he'll be all right,' she said. 'We were there in minutes, so he had the best treatment available.'

Rob nodded. 'I suppose I have to hand it to Jake. He hasn't entirely stopped practising medicine, and from what you told me about the reef accident the other day, he seems to be well up on his skills.'

'I never thought the day would come when you and he were behaving in a reasonable manner towards one another. Wonders will never cease.' She smiled. 'Still, I imagine it must be good news for you with this film project he has in mind?'

'It is. It came completely out of the blue…I

wasn't expecting that. I've been working on ideas all afternoon…there are just a few details I need to think about.'

'I'll leave you to it, then. I'm expecting Grace and the children to arrive within the next couple of hours, and I want to have supper ready for them.'

She went into the kitchen to start preparations. The sun was setting as she laid the table, out on the deck, lighting up the sky with a huge golden orb. Grace arrived just in time to see it, and the children ran excitedly into the garden to take it all in. Their dog, a black border collie, followed them, barking in ecstasy at his new surroundings and wagging his tail to signal that everything in his world was great.

'Everything's red and gold,' Cassie said. 'It's beautiful, Lacey.'

'I think the sky's on fire,' Tom decided. 'The sun's caught the trees and it's 'sploded all over the place.'

'It certainly looks that way, doesn't it?' Lacey

put an arm around her nephew and together they looked up at the sky.

Grace laughed. 'I don't think we need call the fire service just yet,' she said. 'Why don't you children go and explore the garden for a bit while Lacey and I talk? Don't go too far, mind… the orange grove will be far enough. And your supper's ready, so don't be long.'

They ran off, with the dog, Toby, following them, running round in circles, darting this way and that until he was sure where Tom was headed. Tom went to investigate the undergrowth at the far end of the garden, where tree branches hung down and made a convenient den.

Lacey sat with Grace on the deck. They sipped iced drinks, and shared the food that Lacey had set out on the table. There was melon, corn cakes with a variety of meat and vegetable fillings, southern fried chicken and salad.

'Isn't Rob joining us?' Grace asked, savouring

the chicken and washing it down with chilled white wine.

'I think he's working on something,' Lacey told her. 'When he's working he gets so absorbed in what he's doing that everything else falls by the wayside. I took him a tray of food… I doubt we'll see anything more of him tonight.'

Grace smiled. 'At least he stopped long enough to say hello.'

'True.' Lacey sampled the crispy lettuce and red peppers. 'We should plan some outings for you now that you're down here. We could try a trip in a glass-bottomed boat—I expect the children will love that.'

'Yes, they will, if Tom can stay still long enough and not fall overboard,' Grace said with a meaningful look in his direction. 'He's a terror these days…into everything. I'm having a job keeping a lid on him…he's so exuberant.'

She said it with vehemence, but Lacey knew she thought the world of her offspring, all the same. Grace had always been serene, much like her name in character, and motherhood hadn't changed that. She had fair hair and beautiful blue eyes, and her temperament was easygoing, with love of her children shining through.

'Obviously, he gets that from his father,' Lacey chuckled. 'They even share the same colouring, with brown hair and grey eyes. Matt was always a go-getter, wasn't he? What's he up to now?'

'He had to stop off in Miami for business meetings, and then he's going to Key Largo to set up the new offices. He's aiming to join us by the end of the week, but he wants me to go over there on Friday to meet up with a few of his colleagues and their wives.' She frowned. 'I said I'd try, but it will be a little difficult with the children in tow. I suppose I could arrange for them to go to a supervised play centre for a while.'

'Or they could stay with me,' Lacey offered. 'I'm not working on Friday, so there's no problem there.'

Grace gave her a hug. "You're such a good sister to me. I love you to bits.'

Lacey grinned. 'Of course, I might not be so keen to offer another time, once I've spent a few hours on my own with them. They were much younger and easier to manage last time I did that.'

They talked for a while longer, watching the sun sink down below the horizon. The children came back at intervals to help themselves to food, and it was only after their third foray into the garden that Lacey realised the dog was no longer with them.

'Toby, come back here,' Grace called. She was frowning. 'He doesn't usually stray far from Tom's side. I hope he hasn't managed to get himself caught up in the mangroves. Honestly, sometimes that dog is every bit as inquisitive as Tom. He's always getting into scrapes.'

The children went off in all directions, calling the dog, but even though they waited a while, he didn't return.

'I'll go and look for him,' Lacey told Grace. 'Let me have his leash so that I can bring him back. Do you want to stay here with the children? I'm a bit more familiar with the layout of the place. Anyway, he might come back to you while I'm off searching.'

'Yes, that's true.' Grace handed over the leash. 'The children can go and set things out in their room.'

'I'm going with you,' Tom said, looking at Lacey. 'I want to see Toby. He doesn't know his way around and he might be frightened.'

Grace nodded. 'All right. You go with Lacey. I'm sure he's just enjoying the sights and smells around here. I'll go and help Cassie unpack.'

Lacey and Tom hurried off in search of the dog. They called him and shone torches into shadowy corners, but he wasn't anywhere to be seen. Then they heard a faint yelp, followed by a barrage of excited barks.

'The sound's coming from over there,' Lacey

said, turning towards the woods. 'He's probably found a gecko, or something like that.'

'Or it might be a baby turtle near the water.' Tom's grey eyes lit up. 'Toby flips them over on their backs so they can't go away. I think he wants to play with them, but they just wave their legs in the air and I have to turn them over again.'

'I can see Toby's a dog to be reckoned with,' Lacey murmured. Two of a kind, wasn't that how Grace had put it?

'Let's go and see what he's up to, shall we?' They walked quickly in the direction of the noise, but Lacey was dismayed to find that Toby had followed a trail that led unswervingly onto Jake's land. There was a break in the fence where he must have slipped through, and as they approached the border between the two properties, the barking became louder.

Then Lacey heard Jake's voice. 'Stay there,' he said in a sharp tone, and for a moment she thought he was talking to her, until she realised that he couldn't possibly see her through the greenery.

'*Leave it*, I said. *Stay.*' Jake was beginning to sound exasperated. 'Don't you know any commands at all? *Sit.*'

Lacey ventured through the gap in the fence, lifting the wire so that Tom could follow. They walked along a winding path until they came upon a small copse, and beyond that was a cultivated area, filled with flowering shrubs whose fragrance floated on the air.

Hibiscus petals lay all around among the trampled debris of several shrubs and Jake was standing on a crazy-paving path, glowering at the dog. Toby, though, appeared to be completely nonchalant about the situation. He was far more interested in a green iguana, about two feet long, which was facing him. There was clearly a stand-off between the two animals.

Feeling cornered, the iguana extended and displayed the dewlap under its neck. It stiffened and puffed up its body, hissed and began to bob its head.

Toby took a step nearer, and Jake said briskly, 'I said, *Stay*.'

Toby looked uncertain for a moment, panting excitedly, his attention clearly divided between Jake and the iguana. The iguana won. The dog moved towards it once more, and the iguana, backed into a corner by a nearby outcrop of rocks, lashed its tail and bared its teeth. The hissing became more and more aggressive and Toby began to bark loud enough to wake the people in the next county.

Annoyed now, Jake moved swiftly and grabbed his collar. 'You're an idiot dog,' he said tersely, dragging him away from the enemy and putting a healthy distance between them. 'Carry on like that and you'll end up at the vet's surgery with teeth marks all over your foolish hide.'

'He's not an idiot!' Tom exclaimed in an indignant tone. 'You're nasty. I don't like you.'

'Really?' Jake's gaze focussed on the boy. 'I take it this is your dog?'

'Yes, he is. You're a bad man. You shouted at my dog. He doesn't like being shouted at.'

'And I don't like my shrubs being trampled and eaten and my fences broken down,' Jake answered briskly.

Lacey watched the new stand-off between man and boy. The iguana, she noticed, had slipped away into the night once the danger was over.

'Tom,' she said quietly, as she clipped the leash to the dog's collar, 'I think Toby might have been hurt if Jake hadn't stopped him.'

'I still don't like him,' Tom answered, his face screwed up into a belligerent scowl.

Jake looked at Lacey, frustration showing in his taut features. She made a faint grimace.

'He was trying to keep Toby away from the iguana,' she tried again, looking at Tom. 'Iguanas are fine unless they're cornered, but if they feel threatened they might attack.'

'I don't care about that,' Tom said in a fierce

tone. 'He said Toby's an idiot and he said he doesn't know anything.' He stabbed a finger in the air towards Jake. '*He's* the one who doesn't know anything. Toby doesn't eat flowers. *Iguanas* eat flowers.'

'Do they?' Lacey frowned.

'Duh!' Now Tom was exasperated, and Lacey tried to hide a smile. She turned away slightly but Jake caught her expression and a glimmer of amusement showed in his eyes. He began to relax and his shoulders lost their stiffness.

'I'm sorry about this,' Lacey told him. 'We'll keep Toby under control from now on, I promise, and I'll fix the broken fence.' She hesitated. 'I'd better get back. They'll be wondering what's happening.'

He nodded. 'Okay.'

She turned and started to walk away.

'I don't like him,' Tom muttered, giving his dog a hug. 'I love Toby and *he's* a bad man.'

CHAPTER EIGHT

'DID you manage to fix the break in the fence?' Grace asked. 'I know you were up and about bright and early this morning.'

Lacey nodded. 'I made a temporary repair. There are still several other gaps in the boundary fence, but none of them lead onto Jake's land, thank goodness. They mostly go towards the woods and the mangroves.' She folded laundry and put it into a basket. 'I've arranged for someone to come and do the repairs for me, but he can't manage it until next week.'

'We'll have to keep an eye on Toby,' Grace murmured, 'and if we go into the woods we'll have to make sure he's kept on a leash.'

'Yes…we need to be careful with the deer out there. They wander about freely, and I suppose he could startle them and cause a few problems.'

Perhaps it was a deer that had trampled the boundary line and had made her fearful the other night. Lacey's brow knotted. The whole incident still nagged in a corner of her mind, but for now she tried to push it aside. The plain fact was she had to get used to that sort of thing if she was to live on contentedly in this house.

'Tom's still grumpy about the neighbour… though I suppose you can't blame Jake for re-acting the way he did, with his shrubs mangled and a strange dog invading his property.' Grace was ironing T-shirts for the children. Tom had already managed to cover two shirts with grass stains, twigs and sap from various plants, and he'd only been here for a few hours.

'I think the problem was that Jake had other things on his mind, or he might have been a bit more amenable. He'd had a bad day, going out to the diver who was sick, and it perhaps wasn't the best of times for Toby to decide to break in and challenge the iguana. We're very lucky things ended the way they did.'

Grace nodded. 'I suppose so.' She put the T-shirts to one side and switched off the iron. 'Shall we take a walk through the woods this morning, and see if any of the deer are roaming about?' She smiled. 'Cassie wants to try out her new camcorder—I'm sure she thinks she's going to work in the film industry like Rob one of these days.'

Lacey smiled. 'Yes, I heard Rob giving her a few tips before he left for his meeting with Jake.' She looked fondly towards the children, who were playing tag outside in the garden. 'She was fascinated, and he said he'd take a look at anything she videoed while she was here.'

'Then he's made a friend for life. Cassie's very loyal, once she's made up her mind about someone.'

They set off for the woods half an hour later, with Tom and Toby leading the way and Cassie aiming the camera at everything that moved. Beyond the woods were the mangrove swamps, where small, reddish-brown deer fed on their leaves, and supplemented their diet with palm berries.

'Look, Mum,' Cassie said in a hushed voice, 'there's a fawn. Isn't he lovely?' She captured his image on camera. He was tiny, with long, spindly legs and white markings.

'He's gorgeous,' Grace agreed. She laid a restraining hand on Tom's shoulder. 'Don't go too close, because the daddy deer will protect his family. He's watching us, to see what we'll do.'

'They've got funny white tails,' Tom said, watching the fawn graze on the edge of the group. He patted Toby's head while his other hand held more tightly to the leash. 'You can't go near them. They've got great big antlers and they might hurt you.' Toby whined softly in response.

Later, they walked back through the trees to

where rocks jutted out against the skyline. There were lots of craggy inlets here, overgrown by ferns and other vegetation, and Tom and Cassie went to explore the numerous crevices along the way.

'They're like little dens,' Tom shouted. 'Can we play here?'

'Perhaps another day, when we don't have Toby with us,' Grace answered. 'He's probably getting thirsty, and we should be starting back now.'

Rob was at the house when they returned some half an hour later. Jake was with him, going over the film schedules that Rob had worked out, and as soon as Tom saw him his mouth flattened in an expression that said he was ready for battle.

'You're that man who shouted at my dog,' he said, his eyes accusing him.

Jake's gaze was rueful. He nodded. 'You're right. I'm sorry about that. He wouldn't stay where I told him and I was afraid he was going to be hurt.'

'Well, you still shouldn't shout.' Tom was obviously not ready to be placated.

'No. I shouldn't.'

Jake looked Tom in the eye, gauging his response, while Tom returned the gaze in equal measure.

'You don't know much about dogs, do you?' Tom was frowning.

'No, I don't.'

'And you don't know much about iguanas either.'

'That's true.' Jake gave him a thoughtful look. 'I wondered who'd been eating my hibiscus flowers. I guess they make a good meal for an iguana, don't they?'

Tom grinned. 'Yeah… They ate all my mum's flowers, back home. She was mad as mad.'

Jake chuckled. 'I'll bet she was.' He glanced briefly at Rob, who was busy keying things into the computer. 'Are you okay with sorting all that if I leave you to it?'

'I'm fine.'

'Good.' Jake looked back at Tom. 'I want to make a peace offering,' he said. 'How about you all come over to my place and spend the afternoon in the pool? If your mother and Lacey agree, of course.'

Tom thought about that. He frowned. 'Will Toby be able to come as well?'

Jake nodded. 'Of course. He'll be the guest of honour.'

Tom gave a beaming smile and turned to look at his mother. 'Can we, Mum? Can we go and play in the pool? It's really hot and it'd be awesome to go in the water.'

Grace glanced at Lacey. 'What do you think? Do we have plans for this afternoon?'

Lacey shook her head. 'Sitting by the pool sounds fine by me.'

'Then that's settled.' Jake smiled. 'I'll see you over there as soon as you've had time to get yourselves organised.' He glanced at Rob. 'What about you, Rob? Are you going to join us?'

Rob shook his head. 'I'll give it a miss, thanks. Work to do.'

'Okay, I'll leave you to it, then.'

Lacey watched Jake walk away. There was a spring in his step, and she was pleased to see that he had bounced back from his dejected mood of the day before and was now his usual self.

She went with Grace to put on a swimsuit, topping it with a wrap-around beach dress that would keep the sun from burning her skin. The thought of spending time with Jake was already making her pulse quicken and causing nervous excitement to pool in her abdomen.

'You like him, don't you?' Grace asked, as she tied up her fair hair in a soft, cotton-covered band. 'I can see it in your eyes when you try not to look at him.'

Lacey gave a husky laugh. 'Is it that obvious?'

'Only to me, perhaps.'

Lacey made a face. 'I was trying to keep it a secret. I don't want him to get the idea that I have any feelings at all for him. If you give Jake an inch, he takes a mile, and I've learned the hard way to be cautious.'

'Well, I can see how you might be worried about getting involved with a man like him. They're used to having it all, aren't they? And we tend to be just one of any number of women who fall for their chat-up lines.'

That was truer than Lacey cared to admit, but she couldn't help but look forward to spending time with Jake. She missed the way his arms had curved around her, and her lips still bore the imprint of his kiss. It had been such a fleeting moment, but it stayed with her, and if she closed her eyes and thought about it, her lips tingled in delicious expectation.

But it wasn't to be, was it? She and Jake would never be a couple. Jake didn't 'do' the family thing, children and responsibility, and all that went along with it...everything that was vitally important to her. He still had issues to work through over putting his career aside for a life of devil may care, and Lacey had to be on her guard. She had been hurt once, and it was all too clear that she could be badly wounded all over again if she let Jake into her heart.

They trooped over to Jake's house some half an hour later, armed with floats, a beach ball and inflated armbands for the children. Lacey took with her a bottle of sparkling white wine, soft drinks for the children, and a small selection of snacks. She didn't want to feel that Jake was being left to provide everything. He might be ultra-wealthy, but with Lacey it was a matter of pride.

Cassie and Tom took to the water instantly. They played in a shallow header pool that led to the deeper, adult one, while Toby watched from the tiled edge, panting, running up and down and trying to work out how he could get to them without getting himself wet.

'Come here, Toby,' Jake said. Lacey studied

him briefly, her mouth going suddenly dry. Jake was wearing swim shorts beneath an unbuttoned cotton shirt. His skin was lightly bronzed, glowing with health, and she had to fight an overwhelming desire to lightly run her hands over his chest. It made her hot and bothered, just looking at him, and all at once the prospect of cooling off in the water seemed enticing.

Jake, thankfully, was not paying any attention to her just then. He made the dog sit, and then, after glancing at Grace for confirmation, he placed a chew-bone in Toby's eager mouth. 'Go and gnaw on this for a while. That should take your mind off what they're doing.'

Grace watched him and smiled. 'You learn fast, don't you?'

'I guess it's a case of having to, where young Tom is concerned.' He gave a wry smile. 'I've already crossed him once, so heaven forbid I should do it again. Jane picked up the bone for me from town this morning.'

Toby could scarcely believe his luck. Just in

case anyone should try to take it from him, he slunk away, taking his coveted prize over to the grassed area beneath the palms, some distance away. He kept a watchful eye on things, ready to move on if anyone should make a move to come near.

Lacey glanced at Jake from under her lashes. Yesterday's trouble with Tom and the dog had obviously made an impact on him since he had thought carefully about how to make amends. The chew bone was a definite start, and she wondered all over again how much she really knew this man. Everything she learned about him made her heart squeeze that little bit more. It would be so very easy to fall in love with him.

She turned her attention to the children. Their shrieks of delight filled the air as they tossed the ball to one another in the pool, and after a while, she and Grace decided they could be left safely enough while the adults took a dip in the deeper water. Lacey sat on the edge of the pool, ready to slide down into the water, watching Grace as she swam towards the children.

'Come and join us,' Jake said, coming towards her. He reached for her, putting his arms around her waist and tugging her gently down into the water. As she slowly slid into the pool, her soft curves were crushed against his long, male body, her legs tangled with his, and a wave of heat ran through her in an instant from head to toe. He was lean and muscled, with strong arms and thighs, and his whole body was honed to perfection. The way that his hard frame fused with her feminine softness had a stunning effect on her. It went straight to her head. It was intoxicating.

Unfortunately, Jake knew exactly what effect he was having on her. Flame glimmered in the depths of his eyes, and he held onto her for just a fraction longer than was necessary. Then as he released her, his touch was a fleeting caress along the rounded line of her hip.

It was more than enough to leave her yearning

for more and she berated herself inwardly for her weakness...but the soft stroke of his hand on her body was tantalising, a sweet invitation for her to move closer to him and lose herself in his embrace. Of course, she couldn't let that happen, and perhaps he knew it. Perhaps he'd meant all along to tease her.

She pulled in a deep breath and slipped away from him, going to join Grace at the far end of the pool.

It was a glorious afternoon. The sun burned high in a cerulean sky, and the water cooled her hot skin. She made a deliberate effort to keep out of touching distance of Jake from then on, fearful of igniting the lava stream that bubbled just below the surface.

They alternately swam, sunbathed and chatted about this and that, until the children decided that they were hungry and came to nibble on the snacks that were laid out on the poolside table.

Tom looked thoughtfully at Jake. 'My mum

said you used to go out and find sunken treasure,' he said, sitting on a chair by the table and
swinging his legs while munching on potato
chips. 'Did you see lots of dead bodies down in
the sea?' His eyes lit up in eager anticipation.
'Did you see skeletons?'

'Uh…no, thankfully, I didn't.' Jake was obviously a bit nonplussed by Tom's direct manner.
'Luckily most of the people managed to escape
on longboats or small sail craft when their ships
went down.'

'My dad has a wrecked ship in his fish tank
back home,' Tom persisted, sticking to his
theme. 'There's a skeleton in there as well, and
a treasure chest, and the fish swim in and out.'
He thought about that for a moment or two, and
then confided, '*I* think Skelly was looking for
the treasure and then things went wrong and he
died.'

'It's not a real skeleton, silly,' Cassie said, her
green eyes crinkling with amusement. She was

fair-haired, like her mother, a pretty girl, and wise for her six years.

Tom stuck out his tongue. 'You don't know nothing, Cass. I think he found the gold and the jewels and they was too heavy for him to take back up to the top of the water, so he laid down and died.'

Cassie started to laugh. 'You're so funny.' She danced around and began to chant. '*Skelly-welly lost his jewels, had to make do with jelly. Rubbed his belly, couldn't watch telly, that was the end of Skelly-welly.*'

Tom's expression darkened ominously like a thundercloud, and Cassie took to her heels with a shriek as he started towards her. Her shouts filled the air, and Tom's furious 'I'll get you' rang out over the poolside.

Jake gazed after them in bemusement. 'And they say parenting is fun?' He shook his head. 'Beats me,' he said. 'It all looks pretty murderous to me...but, then, what do I know?'

Lacey laughed. 'They're like this all the time, apparently. I don't know how Grace copes.'

'Tranquillisers would be an option,' Grace murmured, 'but I'm holding out until things get desperate.' She stood up and went to rescue Cassie from her vengeful brother, and for a while their commotion blotted out any other sound.

'Heaven keep me from ever getting into that situation,' Jake murmured. 'They never let up, do they?'

'It docsn't seem like it.' Lacey mused on the problem. 'I suppose the key would be to use distraction tactics.'

He nodded, brightening. 'You could be right. Distraction might be just the thing.' He thought about it some more. 'Do you think they'd like to see the treasure collection? I know most people are interested in what we managed to find.'

'Would they like to see it? You're kidding, aren't you?' She raised a brow. '*I'd* like to see it. I thought you'd never ask.'

He chuckled. 'You should have said...I'd have

dropped everything just to give you a tour. It's housed in the annexe, so we could go right now, if you like?'

Lacey was thrilled by the offer. 'Then what are we waiting for? Just lead the way.'

They all went with him to the annexe, including Toby, who brought what was left of his chew-bone along with him.

'We have a complex security system here,' Jake murmured as he keyed in the code that would open up the door to the solid stone building. 'It's linked to the local police station.' He pushed open the outer door. 'Most of the artefacts are held in a museum in town, but this is the family collection, all together under one roof. My father tried to categorise the finds, so there are displays to do with battle, weaponry and so on, in one room, and other rooms house jewellery, or household goods… There are some religious artefacts, too.'

Cassie and Tom were already looking around, their eyes wide with wonder. 'There's a huge cannon!' Tom exclaimed, running over to it and peering into the huge bronze barrel. 'Is there a cannonball in there?'

'I hope not,' Jake said dryly, 'because if there was one in there and somebody fired it up, the end result could be a bit messy, don't you think? The cannonballs could fly around a thousand yards and do some serious damage.'

'Wow!' Tom was impressed. Lacey guessed a thousand was the biggest number he knew.

Jake stayed with the boy, showing him the weapons on display, knives, daggers and pistols, while the girls moved away to feast their eyes on glittering gold and silver jewellery. Some of it was beautifully engraved, or delicately shaped into bracelets, necklaces or rings, and many of the items on display were encrusted with rubies and emeralds.

'I love this little cup,' Cassie said, pausing to stare, wide-eyed, at a golden chalice. 'It's so pretty, and it really shines. It's like the sun's coming out.'

'It is,' Grace agreed. 'The light from the window makes it glow, doesn't it?'

Lacey was entranced by this collection. The jewels were out of this world, and there was a casket of gemstones on display, reflecting the rays of the sun so that it seemed that a rainbow of colour filled that corner of the room.

In another corner, there were ornamental gold plates, depicting battle scenes, or seafaring exploits, and in yet another cabinet there were silver tankards, jugs and drinking vessels.

'It's amazing,' she murmured. 'I've never seen anything so beautiful.'

'I'm glad you like it,' Jake said softly, coming to stand beside her. He laid a hand lightly around her waist. 'I feel privileged to have these things in my home. There's so much history locked up in these rooms.'

Grace came to join them. 'This is all breathtaking,' she said, looking around. 'I'm so glad you gave us the chance to come and see it.' She frowned. 'Unfortunately, Tom's trying to work out how much some of the gold would fetch on the open market. He's decided you might, at the very least, be able to afford a hundred rides on the go-karts in town.'

Jake laughed. 'That boy will go far.'

Grace chuckled. 'And Cassie's planning a range of designer jewellery for her dolls.' She sighed. 'I'd better get the children home before they come up with any more ideas. Thanks again for showing us around, Jake, and for letting us use your pool.'

'You're welcome.' Jake saw them to the door. 'I need to stay and lock up, but I dare say I'll see you around the place before too long.'

Grace nodded. 'You will.'

She ushered the children and the dog outside, while Jake turned to Lacey and said, 'I have to lock one room at a time. Do you want to stay while I do that? I thought I might hunt out those house plans for you?'

'Okay.' She waved to Grace. 'You go ahead. I'll catch up with you in a few minutes.'

Jake turned the key in the lock and set the alarm before walking to the next room. 'I think this is my favourite,' he said, gazing around at the collection of navigation instruments. There was also a ship's anchor and a huge chain, along with other pieces that might have been used to furnish a sailing ship. 'It's what it's all about… the days when men took to the oceans and pitted their wits against the elements.'

'Do you think the sea runs through your veins?' Lacey asked softly. 'Is that why you have all those boats and want to set up your own marine basin?'

'Oh, yes. It's definitely there.' He turned away from the collection, moving closer to her and sliding a hand around her waist. 'It's in the blood. It makes my heart thump and ties a knot in my belly and all I can think of is the roar of the wind in the sails as I race across the water.'

He bent his head and nuzzled her cheek. 'It took me a while to realise what was going on but, you know, I get that same feeling when I look at you. I want to hold you, possess you, and make you think of nothing but me.'

His palm flattened on her rib cage, urging her towards him, the light pressure of his fingers drawing her body up close to his. Her breasts were crushed against his chest, and it seemed as though there was nothing to separate them. She could feel the warmth of his body through the thin cotton of his shirt, and where her wraparound dress lay open at the front, she felt the heat of his thighs against her own.

He slid his hands over her hips, shaping her curves with his hands, and as she took a step backward and encountered the cool surface of a wall, he moved in on her, swooping down on her lips and kissing her with a thoroughness she had never known before.

Her lips clung to his, wanting more, and yet more. His hands stroked, caressed, made her feel as though her whole body was on fire, as though he was all she could ever need, and this moment was where time stood still. They were locked in a time warp. There was only the two of them, and she yearned for his hands on her bare skin, for his kisses to leave a trail of flame all over her.

'You're everything I could ever want,' he said in a ragged voice. 'You're perfect…lush, beautiful, with a body made for love.'

His fingers trailed over her throat, her breast, dipped down to the softness of her abdomen. A soft groan escaped him. 'I need you, Lacey. It's sheer torture being near you every day and not being able to possess you.'

'Jake, I…I want… I don't think…' She broke off. She didn't know what she wanted any more. He spoke of possession and need, and he'd even mentioned love, but he wasn't saying that he loved her… And wasn't that what she needed, more than anything? She had fallen for him, big time, and yet so many things were wrong.

It was confusing, feeling this way, with her brain befuddled and her body crying out for him to make love to her. And yet it would be a mistake, she felt it through and through. He wasn't the type of man to settle down. His priorities were different from hers, and she couldn't bear to be hurt all over again.

She tried to gently push him away, but he was already easing back from her, and a wave of misery and loss washed over her. Why didn't she simply take what was on offer...do as he did, and live for the day?

Only it wasn't her way, was it? Maybe that was why she and Nick had parted, in the end, because she wasn't laid back, reckless and ready to let life take her where it would.

Jake had straightened up, and Lacey tried to pull herself together, pulling her dress around her and tying the belt.

She heard a noise coming from the other room. There was the patter of feet across the stone flagged floor, and then Tom popped his head around the door. 'Toby left his chew bone. Do you know where it is?'

'Um…no,' Lacey managed, dragging her thoughts into some semblance of order. 'I'll help you look for it.'

She glanced up at Jake. He must have heard Tom come back into the building. 'It's all right,' he said. 'You go ahead.'

Lacey nodded and turned away. It wasn't all right. She knew it, and he knew it. She had never felt more miserable.

CHAPTER NINE

'THANK heaven you're back.' Grace hurried to greet Lacey as she walked into the house. 'I was just coming to find you.'

'I was helping Tom to find Toby's chew-bone. It was completely yucky but Tom insisted on bringing it back here.' Lacey glanced at her sister and realised that Grace was thoroughly agitated. 'What's wrong? Has something happened? Is Cassie all right?'

'She's fine. It's Rob…he's not well. He looks as though he's really struggling. He's had to go and lie down.'

Lacey was instantly on the alert. 'I'll go and see him. Do you know if he pressed the button on his hand-held device to alert the technician?'

'He said he did. Does that mean the consultant will get to know what's happened?'

'Yes, it does. The technician will alert him to any major event…plus any change in his ECG will be downloaded directly to the computer. If his heart rate is outside the acceptable boundaries it will sound an alarm so that they can notify the doctor in charge.' Worried, Lacey hurried to Rob's room, pausing only to pick up her medical bag on the way.

Rob had collapsed onto the bed, and when she checked his heart rate she discovered that it was racing like an express train. He was struggling to breathe, as though he had just been running or exercising beyond his limits.

'I know you're feeling bad, Rob,' she said softly. 'Your heart has gone into an abnormal rhythm, and it's much faster than it should be, so I'm going to give you an injection of something to slow things down.'

He nodded, too exhausted to speak, so she went on with the procedure, and then waited for the injection to take effect. Within a few minutes his heart rate had slowed down a little, reverting to a sinus rhythm, still very fast but at least he was out of any immediate danger for the moment. 'You had what's called atrial flutter,' she explained, 'and we need to get you to hospital so that they can start you on treatment to settle things down. I'll drive you over there now.'

Once again, he nodded. 'I'm sorry about this, Lacey,' he said in a breathless tone. 'I'm sorry to be such trouble.'

'Don't even think that way,' she admonished him. 'It may not seem like it right now, but this is actually a good thing. Now we know exactly what type of rhythm is causing your collapse, we can treat it.'

She gently squeezed his hand. 'I'll give the hospital a call and tell them to expect us. Just you stay there and rest. I'll deal with every-thing.'

As promised, she made all the necessary ar-rangements, and between them she and Grace helped Rob out to the car. She settled him in the passenger seat, which was pushed well back so that he could stretch out his legs.

'Are you comfortable?'

He nodded, but looked so fed up that Lacey leaned forward and gave him a hug. 'You'll be all right, Rob. We'll be at the hospital in two ticks, and they'll soon have you feeling better.' She tried to appear cheerful, but in reality she was worried about him. He looked completely drained.

'I've only just come out...of the wretched place,' he said in a flat tone, pausing to gather his breath.

'See,' she murmured, 'you're grumpy already. That's a sure sign you're on the mend.'

She moved away from him and closed the passenger door.

'What's happening?' Jake's voice reached her, and she looked up to see him walking along the dock towards her. 'Has Rob collapsed again?' He was frowning. 'I was checking the lobster pots and saw you getting the car out. How's he doing?'

'He'll be all right, I think, as long as his heart doesn't slip into another abnormal rhythm. I'm taking him to the hospital.'

Jake frowned. 'I guessed as much. You seem to be very concerned about him.' His glance moved over her. 'You still care for him a lot, don't you? I saw you giving him a hug…not something you'd normally do with your patients, I imagine.'

She sent him a quick glance. Why had he brought that up? Was Jake jealous of the relationship she had with Rob? Then she shrugged the thought away. Of course he wasn't. Jake was confident, sure of himself, and he wouldn't waste time wondering what she was doing when she wasn't with him. He probably didn't even think of her at all, come to that.

'I think the world of Rob,' she said. 'I hate to see him looking so dejected.'

She went around to the driver's side of the car and slid behind the wheel. 'Okay, let's get you to the hospital,' she said, sending Rob a quick look. His eyes were closed, and she guessed he was exhausted, worn out by the galloping rhythm of his heartbeat.

She stayed with Rob at the hospital, helping him to settle in, and making sure that she had the chance to speak to the nurses and the doctor in charge.

'We'll take good care of him,' the nurse told her. 'I think he probably needs to rest before the doctor can carry out any invasive kind of treatment. Give us a ring tomorrow, and we'll let you know if we have him stabilised.'

'I will.'

It was late when Lacey left the hospital and started for home. It had been a worrying end to what had started out as a perfect day, and her mind was cluttered with unconnected thoughts. She had missed the children's bedtime, and to-morrow Grace was going to meet up with Matt and his colleagues, leaving Tom and Cassie in her care.

Looking after the children promised to be a

challenge…especially with Tom getting into everything. He'd already said he wanted to go to an adventure park, and then maybe try fishing in the stream, and that was just his before-lunch agenda. She made a rueful smile. At the rate she was going, life would soon become more hectic at home than it was at work.

She saw Grace off next morning. 'I'll be staying overnight at the hotel,' Grace told her. 'I'm sorry it happened like this, just when I was visiting with you, but the dates clashed, and it's an important business meeting for Matt.'

'Don't worry about it. We still have several days left to be together…even though I'm going to be working later this week, we'll have the afternoons and evenings.' Lacey smiled. 'Go off and enjoy yourself. The children will be fine with me. I'm planning on taking them horse riding…or rather pony trekking as we would have called it at home, something nice and leisurely to calm Tom down a bit.'

'You'll be lucky,' Grace laughed. 'See you.'

Lacey went back into the house. She prepared breakfast for the children, and as she was adding the last few slices of toast to the rack, there was a knock on the kitchen door.

She went to open the door to Jake. 'Hi, come in,' she said. 'You're in luck—I've just made a fresh pot of coffee.'

Tom, who was still learning how to do certain things, picked up a slice of toast and began to slather strawberry preserve all over it.

'You're supposed to put butter on it first,' Cassie pointed out in a superior, big-sister voice.

'Ah well.' Tom shrugged as though it didn't matter, waved the toast nonchalantly in the air and promptly lost his grip on it. The toast went flying across the room and landed messy side down on the floor.

Both children jumped down from their seats to inspect the damage.

'Are you sure I haven't come at a bad time?' Jake asked, watching what was going on.

'Quite sure,' Lacey answered. 'It's pretty much like this all the time.'

'Hmm.' He bent down and retrieved the toast from a small fist, just as Tom was debating whether it was fit to be eaten. 'I think not,' he said. 'Try cleaning the floor with a paper towel.'

Tom thought about that, and then nodded. 'Okay.' For once, he was being amenable, and that was enough to give Jake cause to stop and think. His glance narrowed on the boy.

'You're up to something,' he said.

'No, I'm not.'

'Yes, you are.'

'Aren't.'

Tom wiped the strawberry preserve off the floor and then, with a gleeful expression, as quick as a flash, headed towards his sister, armed with the sticky paper towel. Cassie shrieked and ran out of the room, followed by Tom, and in turn by the dog.

'Lord help me,' Lacey said. 'I have twenty-four more hours of this.'

Jake laughed. 'I thought I was the one who couldn't cope with family life.'

She sighed. 'Grace makes it look so easy. I guess I'm just a beginner…' She went to the inner doorway and called after the children, 'If you children aren't sitting at this table eating your breakfast in two minutes, there will be no horse riding. Tom, put that paper towel in the bin and go and wash your hands.'

The youngsters trooped back into the kitchen just a short time later, angel faced, with butter-wouldn't-melt-in-the-mouth expressions. Cassie buttered a slice of toast, adding preserve, and handed it to Tom, who accepted it without comment.

'Are we going horse riding?' he asked, between mouthfuls, looking at Lacey.

She nodded. 'Yes, provided you both behave yourselves. No more fighting.'

He gave his sister a considering look, and clearly he was going to have trouble with that, but for the moment he clamped his lips shut and stared thoughtfully into space.

Jake gave a soft chuckle and turned towards Lacey. 'I think you have the magic touch.' He pulled up a stool by the breakfast bar and sat down. 'I didn't give you the house plans yesterday…they sort of fell by the wayside with Tom turning up at the annexe and Rob going into hospital…so I brought them with me today.'

'That's great,' she said. 'I'll be interested in looking them over. Help yourself to toast and croissants. I'll get you a coffee.'

When she had finished her own breakfast, and the children had gone to play in their room, she pored over the plans with Jake. They were beautifully drawn, perfect in every detail, and she saw that Jake's grandfather had included the natural formations of rock at the edges of her property, showing the location of small caves and inlets. The channel of water ran alongside, and it was plain to see that since the plans had been drawn the mangroves had pushed further out into the water. There were even plans for an additional building on the south side, close to Jake's boundary.

'My grandfather planned to build a boat-house,' Jake murmured, 'but other things were more important at the time. Then, when he moved to my place, there was one already in existence.'

'Your grandfather must have been a great man…he never once gave up on his plans to find the shipwrecks, did he?'

'No, he didn't. And he inspired my father with the same dream, so in the end all his hard work paid off. The only regret he had was not being able to buy back this place. He wanted to keep the family together, all living on the one large estate, and after he died my father became fixed on the same idea. As I said before, they made several attempts to buy it back.'

He looked around the kitchen. 'My mother loved living here, bringing up my brother and me. She never really settled at the big house…

maybe because it is so big, or perhaps because we shared it with the grandparents. Don't get me wrong, we all got along really well—but she yearned for this place where we had been so happy together as a small family. She shared my grandfather's dream of getting it back one day.'

Lacey glanced at him. 'And that's why you keep offering to buy me out? It's not just the commercial interest, is it, with the plans to extend the fruit production? It's the sentiment—the fact that your grandparents and your parents wanted it brought back into the fold.'

He nodded. 'I know it must seem hard for you to understand. It's just that my grandfather put every brick and piece of timber in place, and everything he did was a work of craftsmanship. My father knew that, and it was a huge wrench for him to have to sell up…the only reason he did it was because my grandfather was so convinced we were near to finding the location of the wrecks. Without the money from the house, we couldn't have funded the extra expeditions that were needed.'

She put the plans to one side and looked at him. 'Jake, I know what you're asking of me, but you have to understand that Grace and I have memories tied up in this place, too. My mother planted trees and shrubs in the garden, fledgling trees that have grown to become mature, beautiful specimens. I look at each one and I see her handiwork, her vision of what the garden would eventually become.'

She pressed her lips together briefly. 'My father dug out the fishpond and built the rockery. I remember him spending hours fiddling with the pump and the filter for the water fountain until he had it working just right. He used to grumble every time it blocked up, but the truth was the fishpond was his pride and joy. He built a wooden bench so that he and my mother could sit by the pond of an evening and watch the fish swimming about. When the water lilies were in bloom, my mother was entranced. She loved it.'

Jake made a rueful smile. 'I do understand how you feel…but your parents also had a house in the UK and yet you managed in the end to part with that, didn't you? Are you really so fixed on staying here?'

She nodded, her features tightening a fraction. 'Even more so now that my brother-in-law is setting up an office in Key Largo. Grace mentioned that they're looking to buy a house halfway between there and here, which means we'll be only a few minutes' drive from one another.' She made a restless movement, shifting in her seat. 'Besides, I don't want to uproot myself again. There's been too much upheaval in my life just lately. I'm just beginning to find my feet again.'

She frowned. 'I don't know why you keep asking me to sell up. You don't need this place. It's just one more prize that you want to add to your collection. It seems to me that it's all

part and parcel of the way you live your life…
partying, indulging yourself and living for the
moment. You're used to having everything go
your way, and you're not prepared to let anyone
say no to you. You don't really care about how
your wishes affect other people. Well, I'm sorry,
Jake, but you've lost out this time. This is my
house now, and my memories are bound up in
it and they are just as important to me as yours
are to you. I'm not prepared to give it up.'

'Is that really how you think of me…as a self-
indulgent waster?' He made a brief grimace,
and then studied her thoughtfully for a moment
or two. 'I'd hoped for more, but I guess it isn't
to be.'

She sucked in a deep breath. Had she gone
too far? But surely it had to be said? He had to
realise once and for all that he couldn't have
his own way. She couldn't back down.

His expression was a little sad, resigned perhaps, and full of regret. 'Anyway, I had to try
just one more time.' His mouth flattened. 'Keep

the plans. They're just copies—I have the originals.'

He glanced towards the inner door as the children clattered down the stairs. He seemed to brace himself. 'It sounds as though the monsters are on the move. Horse riding, you said, didn't you? Sounds good.'

'Yes. I found a place not too far away that gives riding instruction and allows horseback riding along specially designated trails.'

'I'm sure you'll have a great time.'

She nodded. Despite the tension that had sprung up between them it was on the tip of her tongue to ask him to join them. She didn't want him to leave. The thought of spending the day with him was suddenly uppermost in her head…but doubts filled her mind and held her back. He persisted in asking her about the house, and now that he had been thwarted, how could she know that he wouldn't still do everything in his power to get what he wanted? Would that include trying to frighten her away? Who was the intruder who had come on to her property late at night? She remained silent.

'I have to leave,' he said, after a moment or two. 'I have to go into town on business.' Unexpectedly, he leaned towards her, wrapping his arms around her, and dropping a kiss on to her soft lips. 'It means I'll probably be staying there for a couple of days…so maybe I'll be back on Sunday morning.' He ran his hands lightly over her spine, lingering to stroke the swell of her hips, and causing a ricochet of sensation to surge throughout her body.

It was as though he was reluctant to leave, reluctant to let go, and yet there was something more…a tinge of disappointment, perhaps, that things had not gone the way he wanted? She had the strangest feeling that he was saying a final, for-ever goodbye. It felt as though something had irrevocably changed between them.

He sighed as children's voices sounded in the hallway. 'I'd better go. Bye, Lacey,' he said.

Then he moved away from her and went out the

way he had come, through the kitchen door and along the path towards the dock. Lacey stared at the empty space where he had been. She was hit by a wave of desolation. She wouldn't see him until Sunday morning? It was all so confusing… she wanted him, and yet she wasn't at all sure that she could trust him.

Life seemed bleak all at once. Why was she so smitten by him? How was it he had he managed to break through her defences and leave her floundering this way?

With an effort, she pulled herself together. She cleared away the breakfast dishes and rounded up the children. Then they all trooped off to find the riding stables, and spent the rest of the morning wandering along wooded paths, enjoying the sight of birds and waterfowl that nested by the side of streams along the way.

In the afternoon they returned to the house and later that day they took Toby with them into the woods. 'He keeps wanting to run off and sniff things,' Cassie said. She was holding his leash, but now she tugged him back from a craggy rock that was overgrown with wild grasses and ferns.

'He can perhaps smell the scent of another animal that's been around there,' Lacey said. She couldn't see anything amiss, except for a few broken twigs and a place where the vegetation had been torn away from the rock. Perhaps birds had been pulling at the dried grasses to add to their nests. Cassie was right, though, the dog was unnaturally drawn to the area.

'Anyway,' she added, 'let's head for home, and supper. There'll be just enough time for you to play before bedtime.'

The children were both content to settle down in the room they shared, later that day, except for Tom wanting to know if he could have Rob's room now that he was in hospital.

'No, because he'll be back as soon as they've made him better,' Lacey told him. They had stopped by the hospital for a quick visit at lunchtime, and she learned that the consultant was to do a heart procedure the following day.

'It's what they call an ablation,' she told Rob. 'The consultant will use radio-frequency energy to destroy the abnormal electrical pathway in the heart tissue. You won't feel it. You'll be sedated and given a local anaesthetic.'

Rob seemed content with all that. 'I just want to get it over with so that I can get on with my life,' he said.

An hour later, with the children finally settled for the night, Lacey watched TV for a while, and then, as darkness fell, she decided it was time to let Toby out for his night-time survey of the garden. 'I'm letting you go off the leash, so don't you go wandering off,' she warned him.

Toby panted eagerly and then ignored her words completely. He sped off, like a grey-hound released from the starting gate, towards the orange grove, disappearing among the trees and leaving Lacey to wonder what on earth had become of him.

When he still hadn't returned some five minutes later, she went back into the house to fetch his leash and a torch. At least the children were fast asleep, so they wouldn't miss her while she chased after the dog.

'Toby, come back here,' she called. She waited. Nothing. She called again, but Toby remained steadfastly out of range. Lacey set off towards the boundary fence, shining the torch along the path, hoping that she would catch sight of him.

'Toby, come here.' She said the words sharply, as a command, and then as she stood still and listened to the night sounds, she heard a soft growling noise. She frowned. Where was he?

The growling became louder, followed by a bark, and then another, and another. Lacey dipped through a gap in the hedgerow and walked in the direction of the sound.

Toby was by the crags, standing guard over a rocky inlet, close by the deep channel of water that ran alongside that part of the property. 'What is it, Toby? What's wrong?'

The dog's gaze was intent on the water. His hackles were up, and his growl was deep and ominous. Lacey shone her torch over the area. There were rustling sounds in the undergrowth, a shadow flitting through the trees, and…something that made her heart shudder for a brief moment…the sound of someone breathing heavily as though he was anxious to make a quick getaway. Lacey felt her blood run cold.

She clipped Toby's leash in place and waited for him to settle. When he seemed content that the danger had passed, his hackles softened, and he looked towards her.

'Okay, good boy. I think you scared him off.' Toby looked back towards the water, undecided whether he should still be on his guard.

Lacey gave a shiver of unease. 'Let's go home,' she said.

The incident had left her shaken. After all, she was alone out here, with two young children in her care, and now she felt certain that someone was attempting to trespass on her property. There was no one around to help her out… Jake had said he would be away for the night, and Grace was over in Key Largo with Matt.

A feeling of dread ran through her. What would have happened if Toby hadn't warned the man off? For surely it must have been a man?

She glanced towards Jake's house and saw that the lights were on. That was strange. Hadn't he said he would be away for two nights? But perhaps he had a change of plan, and he was home after all? Should she ring him? Everything in her insisted that it would be so comforting to have him hold her and tell her that she was worrying over nothing, but the niggling uncertainties wouldn't stay away.

Hadn't she dampened any spark of warmth that might have arisen between them? Why would he listen to her after what she had said? And if he did listen, he might simply say that the place was isolated and she could expect this kind of thing, as he had done before. Wouldn't he be secretly pleased if she found a reason for quitting this place? Surely her fears of an intruder would play into his hands?

She frowned. No, it wouldn't do. If she wanted to go on living here, she had to find a way of coping, didn't she? Bracing herself, she went back into the house, making sure that all the doors and windows were locked.

The next morning she took the children with her when she went to see Rob at the hospital. They amused themselves in the play area while Lacey sat by his bedside. She left the door to his room open so that she could keep an eye on them.

'So you had the operation first thing,' she said, cautiously assessing his condition. He looked well, although he was a little pale. 'The nurse told me everything went smoothly.'

He nodded. 'The consultant said he found the exact spot that was causing the problem, and dealt with it. I'll be keeping the implant for a while longer, just to make sure everything's as it should be, but he says I should be fine from now on.'

'That's great news,' she said. 'You must be so relieved.'

'I am. I'd just like to be able to get out of here now, but my blood pressure was a bit high, so the doctor wants me to stay here for observation for a while longer.' He sent her a quick, assessing glance. 'You've been quieter than usual,' he said. 'Is something troubling you? Another headache?'

She shook her head. 'I've been a little worried lately, to tell the truth. I thought I heard an intruder on the property late at night the other day. Then I decided it must have been an animal blundering about.'

'And something happened to change your mind?'

'Yes. Toby reacted to someone or something that was out there again last night. I'm inclined to think it was *someone*, but I've no idea what he was after. I'm afraid he might be trying to work his way into the house.'

Rob frowned. 'I wasn't aware of anything in all the time I was there on my own. Funny it should have happened soon after you came to live there.' He studied her. 'Have you spoken to Jake about it?'

'Only briefly. I didn't mention what had happened—only that I'd been out on the deck late at night. He said we were isolated out here and things can seem a bit spooky.'

'I remember. I know he told you that there were plans for his brother to come and live next door—I think it was the day Jake came to eat with us.'

She nodded. 'That's right. He's asked me a few times if I would consider selling the house to him, and he would offer me over the asking price, but I've always refused. Now, though, I'm wondering if I'm doing the right thing. I don't like the idea that someone might be roaming around the place.'

'Do you think there's a possibility that it might be Jake?' Rob's expression was sombre. 'I know this will sound bad, considering that I've agreed to do some work for him, and he and I were beginning to get along better, but it might be that he's trying to scare you. Asking outright if he could buy the place and offering to pay over the odds haven't worked, so this might be the next best thing.'

He made a face. 'I never thought Jake was the kind of man to do that, and it's very possible I'm doing him a disservice, but we're talking family heritage here, money and ambition. It's not beyond the realms of possibility.'

'No, maybe not.'

She didn't want to admit that Rob could be right, but the thought had edged in to her mind all by itself before this. How far would Jake go to get what he wanted? Did he want the land and the house so badly that he would try to ease her out? Surely there had to be another explanation?

CHAPTER TEN

'How did things go with Matt and his colleagues?' Lacey asked, greeting her sister. 'You look as though it all turned out really well.'

'It did.' Grace was in an exuberant mood. She hugged the children when she walked into the house around mid-morning that day, and even Toby was rewarded with a tickle behind the ears.

'It was lovely,' she said. 'We had a great time. The men talked business for a while, and we women went to look around the new offices— we stopped off for lunch and then did a tour of the shopping centre.' She grinned. 'A bit of retail therapy—exactly what I needed!' She dropped her packages onto the table in the kitchen, and Cassie and Tom dived on them, looking to see what she had bought.

Lacey smiled. 'I'm glad it went well. But didn't you say on the phone that you and Matt were going to look at a house? How did that work out?'

'Oh, it was so good…you'll have to come and see it, Lacey. It's beautiful. The children's rooms are so much bigger than the ones they have now, and there's a huge kitchen. We've decided to put in an offer, but we want to take the children to see it as soon as possible. I'd hate to see it slip out of our hands now that we've found what we're looking for.'

'So why don't you take them today? I'll keep an eye on Toby for you.'

'Are you sure you don't mind?' Grace sent her a hopeful look. 'I hate to leave you two days running…but I really want to clinch this deal. I think we would probably stay over if we do go down there. Matt has to work this afternoon, so we wouldn't get to look around until fairly late. I think he would prefer us to stay at his overnight lodge…he managed to book into a place where there's fishing, so he and Tom could escape for a few hours in the morning.'

'Sounds good to me. Tom has been hankering to use a rod and reel—for my part, I think he'd do better with a net on a stick, he's less liable to swing it round like a lasso, but there you are. I expect Matt will find him a junior version.'

'It's already stowed away in the car.' Grace spooned coffee into the percolator and switched it on. 'How's Rob doing? Is there any news?'

'Yes, I stopped by the hospital this morning with the children. He's fine, except for raised blood pressure, and they're putting that down to a mild chest infection, a legacy from when he was lost on his Everglades mission, I think. I expect they'll let him come home tomorrow. He seemed to be in good spirits, anyway. He was grumbling about his hospital bills and all the forms he had to fill in for the insurance company.'

Lacey was still pondering his remarks about Jake wanting her out of this house. The more she thought about it, the more miserable she felt. She didn't want to believe it. She couldn't believe it. Whatever his faults, Jake had been nothing but considerate and caring towards her. He had shown her his vulnerability and his strength, and all she had done was to throw his short-comings in his face. How could she have done that?

Somehow, over these few short weeks, Jake had managed to find his way into her heart, despite her best intentions to keep him away. She had fallen for him, deeply, passionately, with no going back.

It had happened when she'd been least prepared, and now she was left to bear the consequences. She loved him, but what did he feel about her? Why did he hold her and kiss her and make her feel that she was special to him, if he was happy for her to leave this place? And yet, despite all that, she couldn't seriously believe that he would do anything to make her unhappy.

'I'm glad Rob's on the mend, anyway.' Grace rummaged through her shopping bags. 'I bought some tickets for a ride in a glass bottomed boat,' she said. 'I thought we could all go this afternoon, if that's all right with you? They're doing a tour of the reefs, and I think Tom and Cassie will love it.' She frowned. 'I'll have to tie Tom to the deck rail, of course…it's either that or lock him in the captain's cabin for the duration.'

She chuckled as Tom sent her an indignant look. 'No one's going to lock me up,' he said fiercely. 'I'll set Toby on them.'

'Just kidding,' Grace said. 'But you have to be on your very best behaviour or you don't get to go on a trip again for a long while.'

'I'll be good as good,' Tom said.

Cassie gave him a long look. 'He lies,' she said. 'He's never good as good.' She turned to Lacey. 'Couldn't we ask Jake to come with us? He gets Tom to behave.' She frowned. 'At least he didn't break anything when we went to look at the treasure collection.'

'Jake's not at home,' Lacey told her. 'I went to call on him this morning to return a couple of platters, but he didn't answer. He must be away in town somewhere.' So if he had come home last night, he'd gone away again first thing this morning. She recalled the disappointment she had felt at not finding him there. She wanted so much to talk to him and reassure herself that all was well between them.

Cassie wrinkled her nose and looked at her brother. She sighed. 'Well, I'm not sitting next to him on the boat.'

Tom stuck his tongue out at her.

'That'll do,' Grace said. 'Go and get changed, ready for the afternoon. T-shirt and shorts, Tom.'

The glass-bottomed boat was a wonderful experience. They sailed close to the reefs and stayed there, so that people could take photos or simply watch the reef fish dart about. They saw sponges and turtles, and all the lovely species of coral that Lacey had seen on her dive with Jake.

The children were fascinated, and Cassie had a whole new range of recordings on her camcorder.

The afternoon ended all too soon, and Grace prepared to take the children to meet up with their father and look around the house.

'I'll take Toby for a long walk,' Lacey told her. 'That'll make up for leaving him this afternoon.'

Grace gave her a hug. 'Thanks, Lacey. I'll see you tomorrow.'

Lacey waved them off, and went back into the house. The thought of being in the house on her own had never bothered her before, but now she was besieged by doubts. What if the intruder came back?

If only Jake could be here with her. She could handle anything if he was by her side. She didn't fear anything or worry about what might happen. He was her rock, her safeguard…but he wasn't here, and she missed him desperately.

When the sun started to set, she called Toby, and they set off to walk around the perimeter of the property. No one would risk coming back to trespass on her land now that they knew there was a dog guarding the place, would they? She tried to convince herself of that. But the fact was Toby wouldn't be here for much longer. Perhaps she would go into town one day soon and choose a puppy to keep her company in the future. With any luck he would grow up to be at least as strong and loyal as Toby.

She felt better, knowing that she had a plan of action, but her contentment was short-lived. Toby, on a long, extending leash, had found that very same spot where he had stopped the other day. Cassie had pulled him back, but here he was again, foraging in the crevices in the rock.

He growled, then sniffed, and then began to paw at the undergrowth. He started to bark excitedly, looking around to see if Lacey was paying attention.

'All right, let's have a look at what you've found.' She went to investigate. 'If it's some ravenous creature with sharp teeth, you're in trouble, young fellow.'

Only it wasn't an animal that was causing Toby's excitement. It was what looked like a piece of canvas, tucked away in a fissure in the rock, hidden by bracken and brambles.

Lacey made her way carefully through the sawgrass, moving closer. It was a good thing she was wearing jeans to protect her from the long, sharp leaves. Toby, sensibly for once, stood back, waiting, panting, while she slid her hand into the crevice and tugged on the material.

It took a lot of effort to pull it out, but when the whole thing was finally revealed, she saw that it was a canvas bag. It was dirty and mildewed, as though it had been there for a long time. The zipper was rusted and try as she might to open it the bag stayed closed.

'Okay, Toby,' she murmured, 'we'll take it home and put some grease on the metal to see if that helps. I don't know what's in here, boy, but it's really heavy.' Technically, the bag was stowed away on her land, just within the boundary line. This must be what the trespasser had been looking for.

Back in the kitchen, she set to work, rubbing the rusted zipper until, at last, she gained some movement along the metal tines. She pulled as hard as she could, and eventually the bag gave up its contents.

She gasped. There were at least a dozen flat, gold bars, a gold drinking vessel, a bag full of coins and several pieces of jewellery decorated with gems. They were all in good condition, protected by the waterproof lining of the bag. She stared at the treasure trove, hardly able to believe her eyes. They had probably come from one of the ships that foundered off the coast.

Stunned, she sat down at the table. What should she do? Whoever had left this hoard would be looking to retrieve it, but it had to be an illegal venture, or why was it hidden away?

Her first thought was to turn to Jake. All her former misgivings melted away. She loved him, she needed him and, more than anything, she wanted to hear his voice. Nothing else mattered.

She reached for her phone and keyed in his mobile number. Whatever he was doing, she prayed he would be free to answer.

'Lacey? Are you all right?'

Relief overwhelmed her. His tone was surprised, concerned, but most of all he sounded as though he was willing to hear her out.

'I'm not sure,' she said. Her voice shook a little. 'I've just found something on my land… at the point where the channel runs closest to the boundary. It's gold, Jake. A bag full of gold artefacts…a chalice, gold bars and jewellery. It was hidden away in a cleft in the rock, and I think someone's been trying to get hold of it.'

'Wait,' he said. 'Slow down a minute. You said

someone's been trying to get hold of it…how do you know that?'

'I thought I heard someone the other night, out in the dark when I was on the deck. And then again yesterday Toby was growling at someone out there by the rocks. I just found the bag, Jake…and I don't know what to do.'

'Why on earth didn't you tell me all this was going on?' She heard the frustration in his voice. 'No, don't answer that. Call the police. Tell them you need them to come out there, now. Lock your doors and put the bag somewhere safe.'

'Yes. Yes, I can do that.'

'Okay, where are Grace and the children? Are they with you?'

'No. They've gone to stay with Matt at a lodge. They'll be back tomorrow.'

'But Toby's with you?'

'Yes.'

'Good.' He paused. 'Lacey, cut this phone call and get the police now. Don't worry about the bag. It's not important. Just lock your doors.'

'I will.'

She had wanted to hear his voice, to know that there was some kind of physical contact between them, but it wasn't enough, not nearly enough. When she cut the call it was as though she had cut off a safety line. She wanted him here with her. She needed him to be here by her side, but she couldn't ask him to drop everything for her, could she? What did she really mean to him after all? She didn't even know what he was doing in town. For all she knew, he was meeting up with friends and drinking the night away.

She called the police, but they weren't hopeful of getting anyone out to her right away. 'Is there anyone trying to gain access to the premises right now?' the officer asked.

'No…but I'm worried that they might try later on.'

'I'm sorry. We have so many callouts to attend to. We'll get someone to you as soon as we can. In the meantime, make sure the house is secure.'

'I will, but if I feel that I'm in danger I'll ring you again. You have my number.'

Lacey rang off. She had never felt more vulnerable in her life. She stashed the bag and its contents in the safe in the living room and then started the process of locking up. She was thankful that Toby followed her from room to room.

'Okay, we've done here,' Lacey told him, as they headed back towards the kitchen. 'All we have to do now is check the dining-room doors.'

But Toby was no longer listening. His ears had pricked up and his hackles were beginning to rise. A low, warning growl escaped him, and the hairs on the back of Lacey's neck began to prickle. A cold shiver ran along the length of her spine.

She turned towards the inner door, a feeling of dread creeping over her from head to toe.

'You have something that belongs to me.' It was a rasping, ominously threatening voice.

A man, swarthy complexioned, with black, dishevelled hair, was standing in her kitchen. He was thickset, with wide shoulders and a grim, intimidating expression. His eyes glittered with menace, piercing her like a knife, and his jaw was set in a snarl, as though he would attack her at the slightest provocation.

'I don't know what you're talking about.' Slowly, cautiously, so as not to alert him to what she was doing, Lacey slid her hand into the pocket of her cotton jacket and felt for the emergency speed-dial button on her phone. If she pressed it and let it go on ringing, someone at the other end might at least hear what was going on.

'Don't give me that,' he said, his voice grating along her nerves. 'You took it. It had to be you. No one else keeps nosing around that place.' He scowled, taking a step towards her. 'You're a pain in the neck.'

Toby growled again, a deep, rumbling growl that meant he was ready and waiting.

'You'd better keep that dog back or he'll get a whack the side of his head.' The man moved his arm very slightly, lifting it away from his side, and for the first time Lacey saw that he was holding a lethal-looking baseball bat. Her mouth went dry. 'See?' he said. 'This is for him…you, too, if you don't give me what I want.'

Toby saw it too, and his whole body was on alert now, poised, and ready for action. His ears were back, his tail was straight out, and his lip curled, baring his teeth and showing his intent.

'You're the one who should keep back,' she told the man. It amazed her that she was even able to speak. Her heart was beating so fast it took her breath away, and all the while her mind was whirling, trying to find a way out of this situation. 'You're trespassing on my property and I've already called the police. If you know what's good for you you'll get out of here, now.'

His mouth twisted in a mocking, derisive sneer. 'Do you think I've waited two years to give up now? Oh, no…that's my fortune you've made off with. It belongs to me. Do you think I'm gonna let you stop me? Think again, lady.'

'I *think* you're making a big mistake,' she said softly. 'You won't get away with this. The police know you've been hanging around the place, and they'll be looking for you.'

He laughed, a contemptuous, dismissive sound that chilled her to the bone. He had no fear of the police, or of the dog. What on earth was she going to do?

'Enough of this,' he said through gritted teeth. 'You're wasting my time. Where have you put the bag?'

'I already told you. I've no idea what you're talking about.'

'Then I'll have to knock some sense into your head, won't I?' Suddenly he lunged forward, grabbing her arm, his hand closing like a vise around her. As his other arm clamped around her neck, yanking her back against him, she made the only move left to her—she jabbed him in the stomach with her elbow, a move that brought a soft explosion of breath from him. He cursed and tried to tighten his grip on her.

At the same time Toby flew at him, all teeth and jaws, ready to do as much damage as possible. He buried his teeth into her attacker's leg, so deep and hard that the man dropped the club and yelled out in pain.

Lacey jabbed her elbow once more into his rib cage, astonished with herself that she could find such strength, but the point of her elbow hit home, and she heard the crunch of a rib as it cracked under pressure. Then she swung her leg in front of his, made a backwards kick and sent him off balance.

Harassed, his hold on her weakened, and he stumbled backwards. Toby found another part of his body to cling on to, this time an arm, and the man aimed a blow at him. It should have hurt but, instead of backing off, Toby tightened his grip on the man until he howled with pain.

And then, just as Lacey stooped to pick up the baseball bat and readied herself to lash out, Jake erupted into the room. Without stopping for a second, his hand bunched into a fist and he aimed a blow at the man's face, a cracking, well-aimed blow that knocked him backwards and took him off his feet. Sprawled on the floor, the man must have wondered what had hit him. Dazedly, he stared up at the ceiling.

'Guard him, Toby,' Jake commanded, and Toby obliged with enthusiasm, placing his substantial front paws on the man's chest, leaning his body weight over him and lowering his head to snarl directly into his face, inches away from his cheek, teeth bared, a low, menacing growl that dared him to move.

Jake flipped open his phone and dialled the emergency services. 'We need someone here, now,' he said, his deep voice commanding, authoritative, brooking no nonsense.

He cut the call after a moment or two and looked at Lacey. 'He said they're already on their way…something about an emergency call you made.' He studied her pale face. 'Are you all right?'

She nodded. Just at that moment she couldn't get any words out. The trauma of the incident was beginning to crowd in on her, and even as her fingers made to tighten on the baseball bat to stop it slipping from her grasp, she began to tremble.

'Here, you'd better give me that,' Jake said. 'It'll come in handy if he's stupid enough to make a move.' He gave the man a meaningful look, but it was clear he was going nowhere.

Jake took the bat from her, laying it down on the table, and she stared at him, wide-eyed, the strength draining from her body. 'What are you doing here?' she asked. 'I thought…'

'I came as soon as I sensed you were in danger,' he told her. 'I must have broken the world speed record to get here…it's a wonder the police didn't pick me up along the way.'

She tried a weak laugh, but failed. Her body slumped a little and he caught her, steadying her with a strong arm around her waist. 'I couldn't bear to think that you were in any kind of danger,' he said. 'For the life of me, I can't imagine why you didn't tell me what was happening before this. If I'd known, I would never have left you alone without putting safety measures in place first of all.'

'But it's not up to you, is it? I mean, I have to take care of myself… I have to sort myself out.'

'No, you don't.' He drew her close and kissed her on the forehead, his lips brushing away the tension that was gathering there. 'I'll always be here for you, Lacey. You don't ever have to worry that you're on your own.'

She gazed up at him, wondering what he could possibly mean by that, but her thoughts fragmented when she heard the sound of sirens and of police cars churning up the gravel on the drive outside.

'At last,' Jake said. His gaze travelled slowly over her. 'You should sit down,' he said. 'You're in shock. Leave me to handle all this.' He frowned. 'Just one thing…where did you put the stuff?'

'It's in the safe, in the living room.'

'Okay. Let me help you into a chair.' He pulled out a chair by the table and eased her down into it. Lacey was more than glad of his help because now the danger was all over, her legs felt like cotton wool.

He looked at her and smiled. 'I'll never forget the sight of you ramming your elbow into his rib cage…and getting ready to swing at him with the bat. Way to go, Lacey.'

She tried a smile, but she wasn't really up to humour right then. She was simply glad he was going to deal with the police and take the weight off her shoulders. All the fight had gone out of her and realisation of the enormity of the danger she had been in was beginning to make itself known in shock waves through her entire body.

A police officer pulled her assailant to his feet and handcuffed him. 'Looks like you need to see a medic,' he murmured. 'Two nasty dog bites there, from the looks of things…a painful jaw and maybe a cracked rib. Not your day, is it?' With the help of a colleague, he marched him out to the waiting police car.

Toby watched him go, and then settled down on the floor beside Lacey to watch what was going on. 'You did a great job, Toby,' she said quietly, stroking his soft fur. She checked him over for any sign of injury, but he seemed fine.

The officer in charge inspected the bag of artefacts. 'I guess he picked these up from some illicit salvage operation,' he said. 'We know who he is. He's been locked up in the state prison for some two years. He must have stashed this lot away before he was caught, and decided to come back for it once he was released. Bad move on his part, because from the look of things he's bought himself another long stretch now.'

'I suppose he must have brought a boat along the waterway, looking for a convenient, out-of-the-way place to hide the stuff.' Jake made a wry smile. 'Of course, he reckoned without Lacey and Toby. That should teach him not to mess with feisty women.' He glanced across the room at Lacey. 'I just want to know where she learned her ju-jitsu moves.'

'Chilterns Academy,' she said. 'Year of the millennium. I can't say I was great at it, but I managed to get by.'

He chuckled. 'You did more than that. You were absolutely brilliant.'

She smiled, basking in his praise for the moment, but she knew full well that without his knockout blow and Toby's ferocious protection she would have been in dire straits. The whole episode left her feeling incredibly weepy…not at all the spirited, never-back-down-kind of woman he had tagged her.

The officers left after some half an hour, and peace finally descended. Lacey stood up, testing her feet on the floor to see whether or not things had returned to normal. She felt reasonably sure that she was back on form once more.

Jake rummaged in the cupboards to find an extra-special treat for Toby, and then he came over to Lacey and gathered her up in his arms. 'It's hard to believe what you've just been through, and all without telling me anything about it. I want you to promise me that you'll always tell me everything that troubles you from now on.'

She sent him a puzzled look. 'I would…but you gave me the impression that you'd have me move out of here. How does that fit in with wanting to take care of me?'

'I wasn't suggesting that you go very far,' he murmured, his head bending close to hers, his lips nuzzling the softness of her cheek. 'Better still, you could move in with me. Now, that would be perfect.'

Her eyes widened. 'Move in with you?' Her heart began to race all over again. 'That idea's turned up out of the blue, hasn't it?'

'Not so much.' He dropped a kiss onto her soft lips. 'I've been thinking about it for a long time...' He laughed. 'Well, ever since you moved here, if the truth be known. I just felt I had to have you near...only you weren't at all keen on me and my way of life, were you, so I was on the back foot from the first.'

'I didn't understand...about the medicine, I mean, but I can see now why you would give it all up. You went through a terrible time, and it was bound to make you think hard about the way you live your life.'

Slowly, gently, he drew her out of the kitchen and into the living room. 'Sit with me, here on the settee,' he said softly. 'I can feel you trembling in my arms. You're still not over what just happened, are you?'

'I'm fine,' she said, but she did as he suggested all the same. It wasn't the events of the evening that were causing her any problem, but the fact that he was holding her, and she wanted so much for him to kiss her, and tell her that she meant everything in the world to him.

'I didn't know where to find you,' she said. 'I wanted you to be here with me, but you'd gone away, and I felt as though I was completely alone.' She frowned. 'I *was* alone. I didn't know how I was going to cope. I didn't expect you to come back.'

'I had to,' he said. 'I couldn't leave you, knowing that you were afraid and that you might be in danger.'

He sat down beside her, drawing her into the circle of his arms. 'I didn't want to go away, but I've been in town looking for a building that I can use for business premises. It had to be just right, with plenty of rooms, open floor spaces and offices to one side. I finally found what I was looking for a couple of days ago, and I was trying to set up the facility so that we can open up as soon as possible.'

She sent him a quick, puzzled glance. 'Are you setting up more offices to deal with the salvage operations? I thought you already had a base in town?'

'I do, but this is something completely different. This is for a new medical facility…a welfare clinic, where people can come for medical care when they don't have insurance or any other means of payment. I've been thinking about it for a long time. I have the money to fund it, and I've set things in motion to make sure that it goes on being a viable proposition. It's mostly trust-fund income that will keep it going, but there will be charitable donations as well. I'm planning to work there myself alongside a team of doctors. It's something that's really necessary out here…a lot of people on low incomes worry about how they'll cope if they or anyone in their family becomes ill.'

'Oh, Jake…' She lifted her hands to his face

and gently cupped his cheeks with her fingers. 'I should have known that you would do something like that. You were never really the loose-living, laid-back, live-for-the-moment man that you appeared to be, were you? I could see it in the way you looked after the woman who was brought out of the sea, and the diver who nearly died. You cared so much.'

'At least they're both up and about and living their lives again—perhaps with a bit more care, having experienced such close calls.' He smiled into her eyes. 'I want you to know that I'm getting myself back on track. I'd do anything to have you love me and care for me, and want to be with me.'

She made a soft gasp. 'Did you not know? How could you not know how I feel?' She kissed him tenderly, rewarded when his arms crushed her to him, and his kiss told her everything she needed to know. He wanted her, he needed her…and most of all he craved her love.

'I couldn't help but love you, Jake,' she said

huskily. 'No matter how carefree and uncon-
cerned you seemed to be, no matter that you
didn't want children, or that you wanted me off
this property, I still fell for you. I couldn't help
myself.'

'Is that really how you feel?' His gaze meshed
with hers, his eyes gleaming with a desire that
warmed her through and through. 'I loved you
almost from the first…but there was your ex,
who kept getting in the way, and Rob, who han-
kers after you and winds you round his little
finger. I didn't know how to deal with that. I
just knew that you were the girl for me.'

He kissed her again, his hands gliding slowly
over the softness of her curves, and Lacey could
think of nothing but this wonderful moment, of
being in his arms and having him love her.

'I've been having a rethink about children,'
he said, at last, reluctantly dragging his mouth
from hers. 'I mean, perhaps they're not so bad
after all. And between us we should be able to
figure out how to handle them, shouldn't we?'

She sent him a startled look. 'Children?' she echoed. She couldn't stop her mouth from smiling. 'I'm thrilled to bits to hear you say that, but isn't that a huge leap from having me move in with you?'

'Well, of course we'd have to get married.' He looked at her, frowning, as though he had no real idea what she was talking about, and then light dawned in his eyes. 'I put that wrongly, didn't I? Of course, I took it for granted that we would be married…I just didn't ask the question.'

He paused, giving himself time to sort out his thoughts, and then he started again. 'Lacey, I love you, and I want you to be my wife. I want to wake up and watch the sun rise over the Keys with you by my side, knowing that you will always be there with me.'

His gaze trailed over her. 'Will you marry me? Love me? Be with me for always?'

'I will, Jake.' She smiled up at him. 'Always. I love you.'

He breathed a long, ragged sigh of relief, and buried his head against her breast. 'We'll be great together, you and I, Lacey. I know it. I feel it deep down in my soul.'

'Yes. I feel it, too.'

She ran her hand lightly over the contours of his rib cage, and he tipped her gently back against the cushions of the sofa. His kiss was long, and thorough, enticing her to wrap her arms around him and draw him ever closer.

She was blissfully content. Together they would watch the sun rise over the Keys, as he had said, and in time their children would run through this paradise on earth, secure in the knowledge that they were forever part of a loving, united family.

MEDICAL™

Large Print

Titles for the next three months…

March

DATING THE MILLIONAIRE DOCTOR	Marion Lennox
ALESSANDRO AND THE CHEERY NANNY	Amy Andrews
VALENTINO'S PREGNANCY BOMBSHELL	Amy Andrews
A KNIGHT FOR NURSE HART	Laura Iding
A NURSE TO TAME THE PLAYBOY	Maggie Kingsley
VILLAGE MIDWIFE, BLUSHING BRIDE	Gill Sanderson

April

BACHELOR OF THE BABY WARD	Meredith Webber
FAIRYTALE ON THE CHILDREN'S WARD	Meredith Webber
PLAYBOY UNDER THE MISTLETOE	Joanna Neil
OFFICER, SURGEON…GENTLEMAN!	Janice Lynn
MIDWIFE IN THE FAMILY WAY	Fiona McArthur
THEIR MARRIAGE MIRACLE	Sue MacKay

May

DR ZINETTI'S SNOWKISSED BRIDE	Sarah Morgan
THE CHRISTMAS BABY BUMP	Lynne Marshall
CHRISTMAS IN BLUEBELL COVE	Abigail Gordon
THE VILLAGE NURSE'S HAPPY-EVER-AFTER	Abigail Gordon
THE MOST MAGICAL GIFT OF ALL	Fiona Lowe
CHRISTMAS MIRACLE: A FAMILY	Dianne Drake

MILLS BOON